Me
(Moth)

Me
(Moth)

Amber McBride

**SQUARE
FISH**

Feiwel and Friends
New York

SQUARE FISH

An imprint of Macmillan Publishing Group, LLC
120 Broadway, New York, NY 10271 • fiercereads.com

Our books may be purchased in bulk for promotional, educational, or
business use. Please contact your local bookseller or the Macmillan Corporate
and Premium Sales Department at (800) 221-7945 ext. 5442 or
by email at MacmillanSpecialMarkets@macmillan.com.

Library of Congress Control Number: 2020919568

Originally published in the United States by Feiwel and Friends
First Square Fish edition, 2023
Book designed by Michelle McMillian
Square Fish logo designed by Filomena Tuosto
Printed in the United States of America

ISBN 978-1-250-83303-7
1 3 5 7 9 10 8 6 4 2

For my gray-bearded grandfather,
William McBride
(1937–2019)

I'm different. I've figured and counted. I'm not crossing
To cross back. I'm set
On something vast.

     —"Crossing," from *The Tradition* by Jericho Brown

MOTH EGG:

a) an oval or round object that is laid & contains a developing
   embryo
b) a roundish home from which the hungry sprout
c) a boundary from the living because we are not ready to *live* yet

This is long work. A finding spell
for roots destined to twine.

—Gray-Bearded Grandfather
(Rootworker)

CALL ME (MOTH)

That's what my parents (Jim & Marcia) named me.
My brother got a "normal" name: Zachary.

My mom's sister (Mary)
didn't like the name her parents (William & Juliet) gave her.

She changed her name to Jacqueline.
(Jack) for short.

I've thought about changing my name.
                              Especially now
                                        with no one to really mind.

Given or replaced, names hang to your bones like forever suits.

When I die people will still say, *(Moth),*
she was great at dancing before she stopped.
            She might have gone all the way,
danced at Juilliard, been the next Misty Copeland.

Like I still say, *Zachary was a pyromaniac, which is probably why,*
            with a name like Moth, we were the musketeers of night—
the torch & the moth.

Like I still say, *Jim & Marcia were really into Shakespeare,*
their favorite play was A Midsummer Night's Dream.

Names outgrow you, like a garden left untended;
they don't disappear
                 with the science that keeps our bodies alive.
Jesus is still Jesus, alive, dead & resurrected—
& if we forget, headstones remind us that names
slouch on without bodies.

So even though my name is strange
                 I have to live with it.
It has been with my nerves for far too long;
my name is a thick wilderness
of angelica root around me,
crafted for my spirit.

& mostly because that is what they
(Jim & Marcia) named me.

ALMOST SUMMER (AGAIN)

Two summers ago our car broke in half
like a candy bar on the freeway & we all spilled
onto the pavement as crumbled as sticky caramel-peanut filling.

I broke three ribs & my stomach tore.
I fractured a leg & was gifted
a scar as crisp as the tip of a whip from jaw to eye that I trace
most in summer, when the sunrays make it feel so chapped,
I have to smooth Vaseline over it daily.

It was the start of summer, we (Mom, Dad, brother & me)
left New York to visit Aunt Jack in Northern Virginia.
       Before we broke in half

            we

                 were

                      merging.

All of our beaten bodies made it to the haunted hospital
overrun with figures in white, smelling like
formaldehyde & alcohol wipes.

Aunt Jack prayed & prayed & bit her nail beds ruddy—
but there is only so much prayer & if god takes sacrifices,
only so much blood to offer.

That day there was only enough prayer
& blood for one of us to walk out.

NOW I LIVE A
SECONDHAND LIFE

After the accident & the scar like the tip of a whip
I changed schools to live with Aunt Jack in the suburbs.

I go to a school that is 94 percent white
with only six Black kids—who don't talk to me.

This is nothing new.
            Black kids sealed
their lips to me in New York, too.
I've always been
a passing breeze,
felt but never seen
unless I was dancing.

Maybe here, in this Virginia suburb,
everyone glues their lips shut because
            I don't wear North Face & UGGs. I like girls
            as much as boys.
I don't slingshot *the n-word* so I am not white or Black enough—
I am not something to anyone.

Or maybe here
silence took root because
first impressions matter
& two Septembers ago Aunt Jack,

who is single & after the accident began drinking
too much, didn't buy me shorts that fit, so I had to borrow hers.
I had to roll them up
to craft shorts instead of capris—
I started sophomore year
secondhand everything
            (shoes, shirt, backpack, socks, shorts).
Everything borrowed from my head to the tips of my toes.

It's fine, I don't mind being nothing
to no one, unrooted on every soil
my feet trespass on.

It's fine, it's just
in New York, two summers ago,
the funeral was rudely everything but mournful—
            the birds tittled & tattled & the leaves insisted
on sunsetting over the urns & everything I wore
was borrowed, even my time *felt* borrowed.

So *now* when I (Moth) think of summer
I don't think of Southern sweet tea rotting my teeth,
            or staying with Grandfather for two weeks,
or bikinis & cheap beer smuggled in too-large purses.

I don't think of riding the wind
or lying down in soft grass
twisting clouds into shapes.

I think of candy bars breaking in half.

WHEN I LIVED
IN NEW YORK CITY

I have noticed some things traverse state lines,
        oceans & railways.

Things like, *all Black kids like sports.*
        Black people like fried chicken
& watermelon & rap music & twerking
& being loud.

I have noticed sometimes a stereotype becomes the truth
        to even the stereotyped,
so when I started ballet at five, I heard things like
        Black girls can't be ballerinas,
their legs are too thick & their arms
are too strong, not delicate like willow branches.
        & my friends dropped me like a hot potato.

Instead of playing outside after school,
Mom & I traveled to the best dance studios
so I could flutter my wings & sprinkle
dust on everything, so I could dance
strong, like Misty Copeland—
& be bullied for being
the only Black one in class.

Other ballerinas said,
Your skin is ashy,
dusty like your name.

I said, *My gray grandfather*
says our skin is rich
like the lands
my ancestors came from.

I only ever felt at home
when moving
under the stage lights.

When moving I could fly,
but after the accident that split
our car like a candy bar,
I gave up movement,
                   so sometimes I feel less alive.

(AUNT JACK'S) LIST OF RULES

1. Don't talk about *the accident* . . .
2. Like really don't talk about *it* . . .
3. Praying about *it* aloud is okay, though.
4. Leaving offerings on the mantel for the ancestors is just fine.
5. Always have wine in the house.
6. Always have whiskey under the sink.
7. Never touch the urns—never.
8. Never mourn loud enough to make flowers wilt.

(MOTH'S) LIST OF RULES

1. Don't live too hard.
2. Fetal: huddle, knees tucked to chin
3. Be as silent as a seahorse.
4. Devour lyrics & melodies like raindrops on your tongue.
5. Choreograph a symphony of movement in the mind.
6. Pour bottles of wine & whiskey into the sink.
7. Watch Aunt Jack search for them.
8. Forget the ancestors, they *up & left.*
9. Build a new god out of toothpicks & song dust.
10. Let your hair grow long.
11. Harden while huddled.
12. Don't crack.
13. Don't dance like Misty Copeland.
14. Do. Not. Crack.
15. Don't. Dance. Like. Misty. Copeland.

VIRGINIA: ALMOST-LAST BUS RIDE OF JUNIOR YEAR

Even after two years of riding the school bus, small bumps make me clench my jaw tight. I don't have a car because *cars cost money* & driving in tiny cars sounds like broken bones & torn skin, which means I am the only junior on the bus. So I am basically a freshman. The ride is too long with only my old iPod, headphones & the one downloaded Spotify playlist Zachary and I made two summers ago for company.

I lift my long green locs, which resemble seaweed or Medusa's snakes, over my shoulder & stare out the window. Every house is white & white & white with red brick & white. Every lawn is green & green & greenest.

The two other Black kids on the bus are younger & don't speak. Or they speak, but never to me. They never bothered to learn my name. Which might be a blessing, considering my name.

I guess a girl with a family who spilled out of a car & who has a scar down her face is too fragile to bully & what is the point of talking if they can't stack insults on my chest?

The thing about the white kids is they do what they want & the bus driver acts like he has cotton in his ears. The bus driver looks like his ancestors oversaw brown bodies picking cotton. The white kids slip new names at the other Black kids like nooses each bus ride.

Two Septembers ago, I started here, at this school in the suburbs.
    Away from the smell of city fuel, where basketballs hitting
    pavement are as numerous as the sound of crickets in the
    country.

The suburbs don't sound like anything.

They are just bland—unseasoned. As tasteless as frozen toast.

In New York, I used to fracture my toes in pointe shoes six days
    a week & cherish the bleeding. My gray-bearded grandfather
    used to say, *You dance like magic because you offer so much blood.*

I used to feel tied to the music of the city, even walked to the beat.
But here, I don't dance anymore. I don't move.
I just sit & think
of drifting away . . .
        away . . .
            away . . .

BOY WITH LONG BLACK HAIR
SHOWS UP IN HOMEROOM

His hair is tied in a knot,
   but a few strands waterfall across his forehead.

The homeroom teacher:
   . . . last minute to start school?

Waterfall hair:
   Didn't want to come.

Homeroom teacher:
   Maybe you can make a few friends before summer.

Golden eyes:
   Don't really care.

He taps his pencil against the desk & more of his hair,
   now looking like lava after it has cooled, slips into
   his face.

He doesn't *look* Black or white or any of the boxes.

The pencil hits the table, then the center of his palm.
   Blond & crimped flutters in front of him,
graceful. The butterfly (Ashley)
wants to know if he is a drummer.

He glances at her—mouth sealed shut.
I notice a cut to the left of his Cupid's bow,
thin & red & angry.
& he taps his pencil slower
       & my feet point in my shoes.
I wrap my ankles around the legs of the chair,
strangling my will to move, to sway, to dance—
to live too hard, too much.

I tug my spirit back into my skin.
I will myself into stone.

Butterfly (Ashley) says,
       What are you, anyway?
His hair covers his face again—
       curtain closed.
              Eyes closed.

He just taps his pencil faster.
Reminds me of tap shoes scuffing
wooden planks, or rain hitting
a tin roof.

No smile. No smirk. Just a beat I can't miss
       that hits a note
              deep in my gut, at the root of me.

"SHARED" LOCKER RULES

1. Don't use a locker, because they are not "shared" if you look like me.
2. First day: My books were placed in a neat pile beside my "shared" locker.
3. Second day: I started putting all of my books in my backpack—I felt heavy.
4. Third day: Then I stopped bringing books because—I was sinking.
5. Now I don't even bother learning which locker I am supposed to "share."

FINAL PEP RALLY:
DANCE TEAM

There are six hundred kids in the junior class
        & all of them love pep rallies.
Even the Black kids. It starts with chanting
        our school motto & ends
with the dance team.

They don't dance so much as gyrate off beat.
        I'd say twerk, but you have to have an ass
to twerk,
        you have to have rhythm to twerk.

The choreography is choppy water
instead of wind blowing
through a field of wheat
or graveyard ancestors kissing cheeks.

The song choice is fork scraped over granite
instead of
hands displacing soft dirt.

In my mind I dance over them, the (flawless butterflies), with my green snake hair.

I stomp them each out like cigarette butts & stare all the men to stone.

In my head I live a lot.
In my head I dance a lot.

TRANSVERSE ORIENTATION

Before my grandfather died he taught me
that a lot of what we think we know
   about moths is as flimsy as their delicate wings,
   which sprinkle
dust & death like whispered omens.

Grandfather used to say, *There are no omens, just balance.*
   Balance is what brings about magic.

It's true that my name is often an omen, but not always.
It is not true that moths like light—
   that's a butterfly thing.

The *truth* is it started with the moon,
when there were no flames or torches.
No cars beaming & hurtling down freeways.
Certainly no cozy front porch lights licking at the night.

Transverse orientation means to follow the angle of the moon.

It led moths straight for millennia,
until fire & the tragic lightbulb.

A flashlight shambled a million years of celestial navigation,
   the artificial hue somehow outshining
   the actual moon.

Grandfather used to say, *We light candles because they are lighthouses*
        for the spirits of our ancestors to come sit with us.
We give offerings out of respect.

But what of other light? Like a sea turtle moving
toward spotlit pavement instead of the moon-rippled sea.

Who will answer for the sin of it being easy to get lost
when so many orbs mirage
        the illusion of brightness?

BUS RIDE HOME

Mr. Hardened Lava Hair is on my bus,
which is stuffed. Which reminds me of candy bars
        & fillings falling onto the street.

Seats are not assigned,
but the one beside me
is usually an empty
question mark.

Mr. Hardened Lava Hair eyes the empty space
that everyone avoids & calls haunted because
a few years back a girl had an asthma attack
& died in this very spot.

Kids cram three to a seat to avoid sitting here—
        but I had a Hoodoo grandfather, deadness
        doesn't bother me.

Mr. Hardened Lava Hair frowns at me & blinks.
              Once. Twice. Three times.
        He glances around the bus before shifting off
his backpack & pointing
to the open space beside me.

I nod.

He sits & with shaky hands pulls a cloth with pills
hiding between the folds from his backpack.
He puts two pills into his palm & takes them without water.
   They remind me of seeds
& I worry they won't grow in the way he needs them to.

His eyes close tight. He shakes his head & looks at me again.
He has a tattoo where his neck joins his shoulder
& a necklace that looks like it holds herbs.

Sani, he says softly. So only I can hear.

   Moth, I say softer.

Sani's dim eyes squint at me. *Shakespeare?*

    I squint back. *Midsummer Night's Dream.*

We both tap while the bus jumps
& the flowers bloom as rudely
as they always do in summer.

Sani offers a thoughtful glance.
   Moth.
     It works.
     I like it.

SAME STOP
(SANI LIGHTS A CIGARETTE)

Sani: *Your parents must really love Shakespeare?*
           Moth: *They did. English professors.*

Fancy. Did?
           Don't want to talk about it.

Lonely?
           Meh. You know cigs are death sticks, right?

I am aware. From around here?
           Nope. Then why smoke?

Is it bothering you? I am from New Mexico.
           Yes. Hot.

I know, I've been told.
           Hilarious. I mean the weather.

Sweltering. Why do cigarettes bother you?
           Why clog your lungs when fresh air surrounds you?

I like having a choice.
           Isn't nicotine addictive?

(long pause)

Navajo Nation.
> Black. My grandfather's best friend was Navajo.

Really? That explains it.
> Explains what?

Nothing.
> Nothing?

Do you ever stop moving?
> Hearts always beat.

Do you ever start smiling?
> I try not to.

You don't want to talk about it?
> I don't want to talk about it.

Where do you live?
> With my aunt (Jack), five houses down.

I live with my mom (Meghan), that way, five houses down.
> For the summer? How do you even get the cigs?

Maybe. Magic, Moth.
> Really. Magic, Sani?

Can I call you?
    No phone.

No phone?
    No phone. Just an iPod.

Right, okay. Bye, Moth.
    Bye, Sani.

MOTHS

Blossom in four stages because they are very good at poker
& don't want to show all their cards at once.

egg (harden)
caterpillar (grow)
cocoon (rest)
moth (live)

This is how it goes.

Egg is nothing special—we are all an egg at one point.
Then caterpillar, spotted & furry like a mustache snatched
       from a face.

                   Cocoon is the miracle.

When the caterpillar literally melts, sticky & soupy,
into slop & reassembles itself into a moth.

          Imagine stepping out of the pot as Medusa.
Imagine your DNA holding the secret to snake hair & stone men.

Imagine being prepared to die
just to fly for a few weeks in the sky.

          It's like you are doing so good at living small.
          Almost mastered reining in your ravenous joy,

                                then a boy with lava hair
                                     & a poet mouth
                                       swaggers in,
                                  wanting your number.

                           He smokes when he shouldn't
                                    & always taps,
                             keeping time with his hands,
                             which I imagine are softer
                              than the mist that hovers
                               at the tops of mountains.

That is what I imagine as I fall asleep
the night before the last day of junior year
& for the first time in a long time
I am not breaking in half, in the back of a car.

For the first time in a long time I *feel* my ancestors
& I think of my gray-bearded grandfather
& the magic he taught me.

I DREAM OF MY GRANDFATHER (ROOTWORKER)

It's fall break & I am visiting my
gray-bearded grandfather, who says,
     The long magic freed our people.
His hands plunge wrist-deep into the damp soil
     beneath a willow
that weeps for our ancestors—with our ancestors.

We are in a sacred place, our feet cradled in powerful dirt:
     a crossroads in a graveyard near Nashville.
Here the living & the spirits can match fingerprints
     & lifelines can twine & untwine.

I remember, I am ten & as scrawny as a vine,
     as wispy as the haunts my gray grandfather chants to—
thanking them for their wisdom, praising them
     for their crafty ways & their perfect plans.

It's a long prayer, longer than usual—
     desperate & outlined in hooded notes,
thunder voice & haunting hope.

Grandfather is old; when he is done
my scrawny strength
helps him stand over the hole
he creates in the dirt.

He pours
       the best
             whiskey onto the thirsty earth.

Moth, you must remember this work.
         You must grow in it. You must live it,
Grandfather says, dusting his hands on his pants.

What conjure is this? I ask as the graveyard breeze
        pats my chapped cheeks.

Grandfather bends down again,
        digs deeper into the soil, places my cut nails,
a tuft of hair & a photo of us in the small pit
along with two tiny seeds & a crisp white feather.

He blows smoke
from his cigar into the hole.
        This is long work. A finding spell,
for roots destined to twine.

Oh. Tell me about how the magic started again, I say,
        smiling into the breeze.

Grandfather covers the womb of a hole
& lets the magic get to birthing itself.

He starts: *There is a tale that those who do the Hoodoo work know.*
There is a boat that has a belly
that sags into the sea—it gorges on brown bodies.
   It cuts the waves like a razor through lace.

Boat docks & there is an auction block & souls are tossed
   like pepper across the Southern states.

A new god paler than salt is named & a whip sharper
than black mamba fangs is threatened, but the ancestors,
the ground & the roots work the same.

We hide hope inside the folds of the Bible books;
   offerings are added to tip the odds.
A rebellion, an uprising in the spirit
right under "Master's" hateful nose.

I help Grandfather stand again
& he leaves his work.
At the gate he covers his face
so the spirits won't gossip
about his private tasks.

But a year later my bearded gray grandfather dies
   & Mom leaves her magic when she migrates north to
   New York.

I remember the stories, the roots. Not the work—not the dirt.
   Maybe that is why my family is cursed.

My grandfather was a great conjurer,
      but *even the greatest rootworkers*
can't raise the dead.
So none of his spells are useful to me.

In my head I hear Grandfather chanting—
The ancestors are with you, Moth,
      you are never alone.
            Taught you. You have magic in your bones.
               Open your eyes, open your eyes,
                  I would never leave you trapped—defenseless.

MORNING RITUALS
(LAST DAY OF SCHOOL)

When Grandfather died & drifted
to the other side, he left me a box
of herbs & roots & soil & candles.

He left notes tied like prayers
to the dried roots & even though
I am mad at the ancestors
for letting the car split in half,
I could never be angry with Grandfather.
So I practice Hoodoo still,
because that is what he taught me
every summer in South Carolina
for two weeks.

My mornings go like this:
            stretch, mantra, offerings.

I have a makeshift altar
in my closet with crystals,
roots, photos & candles.

Each morning I place breakfast
on a white plate so the ancestors
can partake.

Then I brush my teeth, wash my face,
powder on blush & glide on lip gloss.
I pack my secondhand backpack,
dress, chew on bravery & spit out

a shell around me.

FINAL DRAMA CLASS: STORIES

I don't know why, with timber trees for muscles,
Sani picks Drama over PE.

Blond & crimped butterfly (Ashley)
        is telling the story she tells all new kids
about how the left corner of the stage is more than just shadow
& crushed-velvet curtain.

        It's where our very own phantom hovers during shows.

Sani's mouth inches up. His bun is tight & neat today.
        It's a traditional Navajo bun.
I know because Grandfather taught me.
His traditional bun is not as tight as his blue jeans, though.

Ashley asks Sani, *Do you believe in ghosts?*
        Sani taps his foot slower. He is always tapping
like he wants to awaken something in the ground.

The line of his mouth seals shut (again).
        Whatever, wolf boy. (Ashley) stomps away.

I like that he tapes his mouth to her.
        I'd like to un-tape it—I want to hear his ghost stories.

Grandfather taught me that Hoodoo has tidbits of Native
American magic laced in it. That our beliefs sometimes whispered

to each other, like Grandfather used to whisper & chant with his
best friend.

The teacher releases us into the hall for "trust exercises"—
        instead I origami myself behind the soda machine,
with my headphones closing me into a shell.

We do "trust exercises" because you can't act if you can't trust,
        just like you can't conjure if you don't offer something.

I can act like my back is an octopus leg & my arms are conductors
of the waves,
        but my reflection in the side of the soda machine says:
the guilty girl who lived.

Grandfather's voice rattles in my head (again), so very close—
(Moth) I would not leave you trapped—
you are not defenseless.

But I am not my grandfather.
I am not magic & bone.

I am littered
with scars
        & limping through years.

I have nothing to offer the dead
that they don't already have.

THE GIRL WHO LIVED

I am sure that is what the newspaper articles said.
I can't know for sure because Aunt Jack
kept all the newspapers out of the house.

But I imagine the article read something like:
Tragic accident,
an entire family except one
bright, brown-eyed girl taken away
on a highway.

Lucky the girl lived,
because she was known
for sucking the juice
from the sun.
So graceful,
Juilliard was eyeing
her at ten.

Lucky that girl lived,
because she wove rainbows
with her fingertips.
She always licked
the chicken bone—
almost glutinous.

That's probably why
she did not die.

She really knew
how to live.

Maybe if I didn't gorge
myself on life,
there would have been some
left in the car
for Mom
& Dad
& Zachary.

SUMMER SONG

I sit with my notebook balanced
       on my bony knees.
I don't eat much anymore & it shows,
so I hide it under big clothes.

Each summer my brother (Zachary) & I would write a song.
       Just the two of us. Something to pass between us
on car rides & vacations.

When it was winter & we needed the feeling
of sun on our skin, we would sing our song.

I can't play guitar.
       Zachary played the guitar.
But I can still write, hum
& if my heart is light enough, sing.

I write my first lyric of summer:
       A gift, an iron
              to smooth the creases that wrinkle up your spirit.

I don't know where the song is headed,
       but that's the best part.
The dog days of summer decide the lyrics—
              as they should.

SANI SINGING IN THE EMPTY ROOM

From my hiding place a voice
creeps softly to me.

A voice low & gruff
& hungry
& hopeless.

I have to follow the sound
& I find Sani, at the piano
playing
& singing
& my feet turn out,
find first position
before I can stop them.

It's not a song I know.
It's a song I think Sani wrote.
He sings, his voice cuts
like lightning through thunder clouds.

It's hard to be what everyone wants
when living feels like haunting.

Mother worries & flinches all the time,
Father busy healing & praying.

Stepfather hates that I was born,
he wants to erase me.

It's hard to be what everyone wants
          when living feels like haunting.

Sani looks up,
          sees me eavesdropping.

He frowns,
watching me
as I fail to string
together an apology
for hearing his song.

He stands,
hesitates
for heartbeat
& leaves.

I FIND SANI BY
THE VENDING MACHINES

Sorry, I say.

It's not polite to hover.
Sani raises an eyebrow.

Side effect of my name?
      I tap my fingers.
I like your voice.

I like compliments.

Sani laughs & tugs
the trust exercise sheet with five questions
from his tight jeans & says, *Shall we?*

He (Sani) answers first.

What is your favorite color? *Earth.*
    What is your passion? *Sometimes music. Usually nothing.*
      What do you miss? *Nothing.*
        What is trust? *Meh.*
          Coffee or tea? *Neither.*

I (Moth) answer next.

What is your favorite color? *Black.*
    What is your passion? *Music & movement.*
      What do you miss? *Swallowing the sun.*

What is trust? *My gray-bearded*
grandfather.

Coffee or tea? Both. With honey.

Sani pulls out a pen & adds another question.

Coffee with honey? Are you writing a poem?
A song. Yes, with honey.

Sani writes another note.

I play guitar & piano. Maybe I could help.
He scrawls his number.

I don't have a phone. (I answer with my voice.)

Find a phone & call me, text me? Please, honey?
Penance for hovering & listening to my song.
(Sani answers with his voice as soft as fall
leaves floating on a lake.)

NOTE SANI SLIPS INTO
MY HAND

Verse 2:

> *a bundle of beer, a bouquet of clichés*
> *because it's almost summer & it feels right.*

His number is scrawled there (again).

I add:

> *I hear you never come empty-handed in the South*
> *& I am nothing if not polite.*

Then I roam into the woods behind the house.
> I beg the ground for the first root Grandfather taught me.

Next I slip back into Aunt Jack's house.
> I slink into her purse,
>> borrow her iPhone
& replace it with the most important root—
High John the Conqueror root.
> I leave courage & cleverness behind
because *I am nothing if not polite.*

EGG

I run upstairs with my prize.
I re-shell when my bedroom door closes.

Safe & hardened.
I pace.

Sometimes in silence
the heated hands of hell reach
up through the floor, ready to pull me
      down
            down
                  down.
Like they forgot me when they took everyone else.

I feel the heat even though I surround myself
with Devil's root (stuffed in my pillowcase,
in my drawers & pockets).

Grandfather taught me it is a root to trip
the feet of Satan & his minions;
he left some in the box he gave me.

I fall on my bed & firmly press my back against the quilt.
I practice the positions (first, second through fifth)
      because if you don't touch the ground,
it doesn't count as dancing.

First position:

> *It's not your fault you lived.*

Second position:

> *Until you are alone.*

Third position:

> *Fault lines multiply.*

Fourth position:

> *So you sacrifice.*

Fifth position:

> *For accidently living, for being so filled*
> *with life, death did not recognize you.*

TEXT I SEND SANI
I found a phone.

TEXT SANI SENDS (3 SECONDS LATER)
Hello (Moth). I was hoping you would.

TEXT I SEND SANI
So, here for summer?

TEXT SANI SENDS
My mom (white) left my dad (Navajo) in
New Mexico 2 years ago.
He was gentle, but busy with healing.
Mom wants me to live here in this white house.
With her new white family.
She thinks it will be good for me.

TEXT I SEND SANI
You offer a lot of information.

TEXT SANI SENDS
You offer very little information.

TEXT SANI SENDS (5 MINUTES LATER)
You also walk like there are clouds beneath your feet.
Your eyes move like you think everyone is dancing.
Your voice is thick & smooth, like honey in a beehive.

It's fine. You don't have to answer.

You can ignore me, honey.

TEXT I DO NOT SEND SANI

The curve of your lip has a nick, why?

I am a dancer, but I only dance with the air now.

Your hair reminds me of the sky before the moon rises.

Why do you take pills?

My brother (Zachary) used to take

blue-and-white pills (for the black hole in his center).

When the pills worked, he played guitar sitting on

       the kitchen counter.

When the pills worked, I'd weave a dance from the melody.

Your name means "wise." I googled it.

They (the entire school) will stop calling you *wolf boy*—

at my old dance studio they stopped calling me *blackie & dusty*.

Eventually they'll get bored.

TEXT I ACTUALLY SEND SANI

I used to dance.

Do you sing & play often?

TEXT SANI SENDS BACK

Honey, you've been dancing since I saw you.

I used to sing often. I used to play often.

TEXT I SEND BACK

Sani, you are always tapping something.
Your voice plucks out notes
even when you are talking.

                                    TEXT SANI SENDS BACK
                                    I guess we are both muffling
                                    our passions, for reasons.

TEXT I SEND BACK

For reasons . . .

I USED TO DANCE

Before the car crash I was a dancer—
I conquered gravity while breaking my toes.
I kissed the ground with every step.

Being a dancer is like your name, though. You can't stop being one
        just because your toes don't fracture in your pointe
        shoes.

After the crash, I am still a dancer, but only in my head.
'Cause dancing feels too joyful, too greedy now.

Dad (Jim) used to run with me every Sunday & Thursday
because dancing like a pebble skipping over water
means your lungs have to be good at catching their breath.
Mom (Marcia) came to every dance competition.
        She sat in the front row recording everything on her
        phone.
I could hear her whispering—*Now that is how you move*—on the
        recordings.

I still go on long runs & pretend
Dad's heavy footfalls echo
sure, steady, and watchful beside me.
I still play Mom's recordings sometimes, on an old laptop,
        when it's hard to remember her voice—
Now, my girl knows how to love the air.

Mom, Dad, Zachary, and I listened to endless songs & stitched
        together
a playlist for the big day—
        the day I would audition for Juilliard. The list grew like
        taffy,
something sweet always strung between all of us.

I have not danced with my feet on the floor
since the car split in half like a candy bar.

I stretch, though.
I sit in the splits.
I lie on my back
&
insist on breaking my toes on nothing.

IF I WENT TO THERAPY, I THINK
IT WOULD GO LIKE THIS

Therapist: You can't *live too hard*, Moth.
Therapist: You can't *live too hard*, Moth.
Therapist: You can't *live too hard*, Moth.

Moth: Then why did death forget me?
Moth: Then why did death forget me?
Moth: Then why did death forget me?

Therapist: *Less living* won't bring them back, Moth.
Therapist: *Less living* won't bring them back, Moth.
Therapist: *Less living* won't bring them back, Moth.

Moth: I no longer drink the juice of the sun.
Moth: I no longer drink the juice of the sun.
Moth: I no longer drink the juice of the sun.

Therapist: I recommend meeting more. Perhaps making friends.
Moth: My grandfather says our ancestors are never gone.

But I don't know enough conjure;
   Grandfather passed to heaven before I learned & now
the devil keeps nipping me through the ground,
like he forgot one of his prizes,
   begging me back down
      down
        down.

REASONS I HATE SUMMER

1. Three months of waiting in a silent shell.
2. I can't think of anything except snapping in two.
3. My scar is chapped & my face tans & it shows more.

Reasons I Might Not Hate This Summer

1. There is a boy who carries mountain smoke on his breath.
2. He has cedar around his neck & tattoo-laced skin.
3. He sings like fog being pulled from the lake.
4. He plays like birds' wings kissing the wind.
5. He lives ten houses down.
6. I don't understand why, but he *sees* me (Moth).

BLACK WITCH MOTH

The largest species of moth is an omen & a blessing—
        depending on who you ask.

A butterfly & a moth both birth the same—
        melt their innards & reassemble.

One pretties the day, the other hunts the night.
        Mom said, *That's the difference between Black & white—*
it's harder to sway your hips when you are crafted to hunt.
I always thought I could be both.

If you're asking me, I'd go with facts:
        Moths came first by several million years.
Butterflies were made from the ribs of moths.

I'd rather have wings that stretch like taffy,
that swoop instead of flutter.

I'd rather be feared & blessed
than be too perfect.

Dad said, *Sometimes you have to dig deep,*
get a little dusty, to bury
the seeds of your dreams.
I don't mind digging.
I'd rather be dusty—

something you can't touch
without getting a little dirty.

I'd rather migrate,
like the black witch moth—
       instead I keep finding myself
in the place I want to leave.

AUNT JACK IS LEAVING
FOR THE SUMMER

She doesn't say it to my face;
she is not that brave.

I don't know if me borrowing her phone
& replacing it with John the Conqueror root
         was the last straw. I am bad like that—
sometimes I take what I should not
because I live too hard
& that is why the devil nips at me.

She leans on the fireplace, screaming at the urns,
        offering oranges to the spirits.

Small hiccups erupt from her lips
like hopeless bubbles popping around the house.

I can't do this. I am leaving for the summer (she screams).
        I need to get away. I can't live with your ghosts (she whispers).

I take the stairs two at a time. I don't let her whip around
& apologize.

I get it. I am the problem.

I hate me, too.
For living & now strangling
myself into living small.

I get that she can't sit with sadness anymore.
        I pace until night drifts in & I hear something
in the backyard. I open the wooden blinds
& Aunt Jack is digging a hole. She is whispering words,
leaving a picture & pouring whiskey on the ground.

I wonder what Grandfather would say to this Hoodoo work.
        Trying to forget instead of remembering your ancestors.
I guess pain does that—it makes you want to forget.

GOODBYE NOTE STUCK
TO THE FRIDGE

I am so sorry, I can't stay.
           Please
forgive

                 me.

DUST #1

I don't forgive her.
I muffle a sob & dust coughs
          onto my brown hands.
My insides
are as shriveled up
& dry as dirt.

I am choking on dirt.

TEXT I THINK ABOUT
SENDING SANI

I am alone & it's my fault.
Sometimes I think I hear things in the house
& sometimes I feel hands tugging me into the ground.

My aunt (Jack) left for the summer.
I am 17 years old & I guess I can take care of myself.

Sometimes I think I will become so paper-thin,
my scar will tear open
                              & my soul will fall out,
filled with stars & sticky as the universe.

I think I might have a party.
I tried this living small thing—
it only took another person away.

TEXT I SEND SANI
My aunt bailed for the summer.
I am going to throw an epic party.

                              TEXT SANI SENDS BACK

                              Nothing. He doesn't answer.

INSTAGRAM PARTY POST

I don't like any pictures of me,
so I just create an image in black & white that says:

      SUMMER IS FINALLY HERE PARTY.

I tag everyone—
      the kids who call Sani *wolf boy*,
      blond & crimped (butterfly),
      the basketball team & the soccer team
            & the football team
      & the chess squad & the debate group.

I want them to trash the house
& for the police to come.

I want my aunt (Jack) to be called.

I want to rage.
I want to be a thunderstorm.

INSTAGRAM POST RESULTS

I find streamers in the attic.
        I make a playlist of chill & funk,
bake brownies & set out chips
that I won't eat, but I want them to eat.
I want them to be stuffed & friendly.

I even borrow a few bottles of Aunt Jack's wine.

    Then
           this
                happens.

                            No one shows.
                            Not even Sani.

I log on to Instagram—
        comments litter the invite.

What a sick joke.
Who would come to this?
I would not be caught dead there.

No one liked the post.
        Not a single person.

I leave out the food, an offering for the ancestors.
I hope they sit & eat.
At this point I'll even take
the company of the heated hands of hell.

THROUGH THE WINDOW

I stomp down the front steps,
       down one

              two

                      six

                            ten houses

& find a large picture window, displaying a boy (Sani),
       a girl, a mom & a dad, like a movie.

It's a very late dinner
& napkins cover laps before
they bow their heads.

Sani is shaking his head *no*
& his mouth is sealed the same way
it was at school.

I can hear his (step)father scream,
       You are going to college for business. I don't care how sad
          it makes you.
       You won't be a lazy artist. I won't pay for that.

I hear Sani yell,
      I don't want anything from you.
       Say something, Mom,
          why don't you ever say something?

She (Mom) places a pill
in Sani's hand.

My anger evaporates like mist touched by the sun.
            Sani rolls it between his thumb & index finger—
blue and white.

He plops
it
into his mouth,

drinks & slams the glass, hard,
                    so hard
on the table.
It shatters around his fingers; blood
                        floods the napkin.

She (Mom) grabs his plate & rushes to the kitchen.
            His step(father's) fist connects with Sani's shoulder
before he heads toward the kitchen.
She (sister) pulls her teddy bear out
from under the table
& places it in Sani's bloodless hand.

Something crashes in the kitchen.
          Sani flinches.
My heart cracks
& Sani hears it, because he glances at the window.
          He swallows, blinks, shakes his head,
crosses the desert between us,
but I am already running away.

AT LEAST THE ANCESTORS
WERE HUNGRY

When I get home the food is still out
            but the colors are dull.
Grandfather used to say,
That is how you know
the ancestors took the energy from the food.

So at least I am not all the way alone.

I go out into the woods behind Aunt Jack's house,
            jacketless, with a basket hooked in the crook of my arm
to hold herbs, roots. A flashlight to guide the way.

Moths slam into the flashlight glass;
they are confused because night drapes
over everything except the light.

Here I am the bright thing,
killing things again.

It is cold.
Like winter has suddenly
sleighed into these woods.

I sit & sit.
Get colder & colder.

So cold, I think of falling
through the ground.
        Until . . .

                        Moth, is that you? Honey, are you cold?
                                        Moth, talk to me.
                                Honey, I am so sorry.

Sani grips me at the waist
& behind the knees, lifts me like air.
I nuzzle into his neck that smells
            of witch hazel bark.
He climbs the stairs, opens the front door,
places me on the sofa, tucks me in a blanket.
I am cocooned.

                        There's really no one here?
                                Your aunt left?

I nod slow, feeling the warmth come back
& I start to shake.

Sani rubs the back of his neck
before untucking
the blanket
to tuck himself in beside me.

TEXT SANI SENDS WHEN HE'S GONE IN THE MORNING

Sorry we both had a bad night.
I didn't expect to see you.
I didn't want you to see me like that.
I am like that a lot. I have some issues.
My stepfather is religious; he thinks I am evil.
Sometimes he ... never mind.
I've given up smoking. You're right.
Sorry no one came to the party.
They don't deserve your company.
Sorry your aunt left.
Sorry. Sorry. I am so so sorry, honey.

TEXT I WANT TO SEND SANI
I didn't mean to see you
through the window
surrounded by glass fracturing like glitter.
I didn't know where else to go.
I think the moon led me
to your doorstep.

TEXT I SEND SANI
What's the tattoo above your wrist?
& where are you applying?

TEXT SANI SENDS BACK
Five finger grass.
I've had it forever.
& nowhere.
I was, but not anymore.

TEXT I SEND SANI
In Hoodoo five finger grass
        tempts others to do your bidding.
I deleted my Juilliard application.

TEXT SANI SENDS BACK
Dreams change
& you know your plants.
Like a medicine man.

TEXT I SEND SANI
My grandfather taught me.
& no, dreams don't change,
we just pretend
we don't want them anymore.

TEXT SANI SENDS BACK
"Summer Song"
Honey, all the clocks are against us,

we've got one summer, I'll do your bidding.
Just tell me what you want.
I'll do anything you want.

TEXT I SEND SANI
Anything I want?
You hardly know me.

TEXT SANI SENDS BACK
Then why do I feel
like the dust of your name
is buried in my bones?

TEXT I SEND SANI
Dramatic.
Five finger grass. Maybe?
I am glad you stopped smoking,
also maybe try out for Juilliard?

TEXT SANI SENDS BACK
Moth. Finding my voice
(again)
is not as easy
as giving up smoking.

I'LL DO YOUR BIDDING

I want to offer Sani some of my spark,
        the thing that kept me alive in the car,
because that is what I need to dull,
because that is what makes it all my fault
& he seems to need more of it.

It's like you play the part of invisible for years
& the egg cracks, revealing something other.
Like when the warrior layers off his armor
        & even clothed, he feels naked.

Just tell me what you want.
        I'll do anything you want.

But Sani smells like witch hazel bark.
        I know that root. Grandfather said
Native Americans taught settlers about witch hazel bark.
It can reduce grief, but it also can reduce the ability to love.

All I can smell is witch hazel when I smell Sani—
        it burns the inside of my nose. So honestly—
I don't know. I don't know.

SUMMER STORM

Thunder rattles the house,
        plucking at the screens,
howling through
feather-thin
cracks.

Something pounds, desperate, at the front door
& I am sure this time it is the devil coming to get me.

I tighten my blanket around my shoulders.
The front door swings open & Sani is dripping wet.

Fists clenched,
guitar strapped
to his back
& hair free & lip bleeding
& eye bruised
& chest heaving
& & & . . .

He stumbles in, drenched
        & shaking & mumbling,
then smashing his guitar
against the floor. It cracks
& his voice cracks,
He said I was sick in the head,
        he hit me (again),

he said I'd never get into Juilliard
with a mind like mine.

        He kept hitting me.

My eyes are wide & Sani's hands shake
as they pour a waterfall of (far too many)
pills into his palm.

He glares at his handful
of (too many) pills,
then at me.

I can't find air;
my lungs tighten,
reading the thoughts
written in his eyes.

I sprint forward,
knock the hopelessness
out of his hand
but not off his face.

His pills spill
across the wooden floor.

I grab him. *You can't do that, Sani!*
    He crumbles into me.

He kept hitting me.
She didn't stop him.

I wrap us tight on the floor
in my blanket,
rocking him back & forth,
not sure how I got here
with this beautiful, sharp-edged boy
whose voice is dipped in spirit & dust,
   who smells like rain & dirt.
& me (Moth) a spark that won't unlight—
a spark that wants to be a wildfire—
     to ignite.

  I whisper "Summer Song":
  I want to suffocate your sadness,
    I want to run away with you. Please run away with me.
  He nods
    & nods
      & nods.

RUN AWAY WITH ME, PLEASE

A road trip is a thing that you go on & come back different.

We were road-tripping before the car split.
     From New York to Virginia.

         & because even in summer, when all things happen,
when in the movies the cool kids love the outcast, I feel guilty
for sparking a little—
for being seen.

& because the house is too silent without clinking bottles.

I decide to be taffy & stretch across the US
     from Virginia to his Motherland.

Because he (Sani) needs
to live & leave
& I think I might,
possibly, need
the same thing
because I don't
belong anywhere
anymore.

WORMWOOD & GINGER ROOT

I stuff both in a flannel bag to hang on the rearview mirror.
      Wormwood: to protect the car, keep it in the palm
of the ancestors' hands.

Ginger root: for adventure & freedom.

This summer I want both,
      I need both.
Please,
summer,
give me both.

Then I promise to cocoon again.

CATERPILLAR:

a) a segmented larva of a butterfly or moth
b) a long road that grows & grows until it doesn't
c) the start of creation; a story of creation

You (Moth) will have to stretch your soul
like an endless story to find your way.

—Gray-Bearded Grandfather
(Rootworker)

UP & LEAVE

If you are going to disappear,
you have to empty the fridge—
        deli meat, milk & yogurt hulked
into the neighbors' trash bin.

Everything must go
except for the dull party food
        the ancestors ate from,
which gets buried deep in the ground
with a few coins under a tree
in the woods behind the house.
        (My subtle way of begging for a miracle.)

House is swept,
        sheets stripped,
                washed & folded into clouds.

Drapes drawn, signaling a close in business.

I think about leaving a note for Aunt Jack,
just in case she comes back early,
        but she didn't bother to say bye to me.

Now that I think of it,
she hardly remembered to say *hi*,
so I don't leave a note.

>   I gather & rebottle the pills
I made Sani spill.
I lock the front door.
>   I don't look back.
>   Steps in new directions are the hardest to take
& it is hard to be sure if Sani is the moon
or just a dumb lightbulb.

Sani is outside in his Wrangler with a full tank,
>   looking like salvation & sin—
in the few days since the summer storm,
he has reassembled somehow.
Ready to string himself across two families
>   from Virginia to the Navajo Nation.

Sani has a shock of lipstick in the center of his right cheek,
>   a fading bruise framing his eye
& an overloved teddy bear strapped in the backseat
next to his guitar, whose crack is now hidden with duct tape.

I have my name (Moth)
& a gym bag stuffed with some of Aunt Jack's clothes
>   because mine are all old & a small flannel bag
filled with crushed ginger root & wormwood,
which I tie to the rearview mirror
beside the bag of cedar
Sani's father gave him.

What's that for? (Sani tugs the bag.)

To keep us safe. (I swallow.) *Cars make me nervous.*

(He nods.) *I like it, it smells like Christmas.*
Wormwood & ginger root.
Adventure & protection. Right?

How'd you know?

I know things (he says, pulling away
& squinting into the sunrise).

I place his pills on the dashboard like an offering.
Sani brakes the car, pulls over,
takes one blue & white oval
without water
before merging back into traffic.
I lick my thumb & wipe the red shock
        from Sani's cheek. I don't know how to
wipe away a bruise.

I lean back in my seat, thinking
it's strange when no one cares if you up & leave.

SANI'S JEEP WRANGLER

I decide the beat-up Jeep is a caterpillar, because that makes
        the expanse of road in front of us
less death trap, more journey.

The doors can be taken off & the wind
        can make Sani's hair more water than lava.

It can make the wind finger across our skin
        as we caterpillar away, hearts thin but ready
to gorge.

Ready to rewrite our summer, maybe even change
        our creation stories. Ready to un-break cars
& thumb away bruises. Maybe moving forward
in this Wrangler will be enough to feel at home
(somewhere), if only for a moment.
Maybe moving forward in this car
will help to fill in Sani's emptiness.

Sani adjusts the rearview mirror.
        We are leaving the First World,
the world of darkness (Ni'hodilhil),
        where the Diné start their journey to the present.

I stretch my legs in front of me.
Who lives in the First World?

Insects & Holy People.

A bee flattens against the Wrangler window.
Are you sure we are leaving the First World?

I am sure (he says as the windshield wipers
clear away the carcass of the bee).

CATERPILLAR

After the egg spills open, a larva waddles out
               & starts to eat a hole through the center of its universe.

Sometimes it nibbles;
often it inhales entire trees.
               It gets as furry & fluffy as a cotton ball.

It inches longer—
building a road of itself
that leads somewhere opposite of home.
It wants to live.

Or ...

An egg spills open & a larva waddles out
               & decides it doesn't want to eat.

It would rather be a larva.
It doesn't want to change into anything.
It wants to exist.

Or ...

In the rarest creation myths, the egg spills open—
          & a moth flies out,
                    then another
& another
          & another
                    & another
& that is called a plague.

LYRICS & STORIES

The best way to get to know someone,
        to get beneath their skin & into the bone,
is to tell a story & offer music.

A story explains who you *want* to be;
        the other shows who you *are*.

When Sani & I climb into the Jeep,
        we feed each other
the only thing we own:
stories & song.

Our "Summer Song"
        is a red string between us.

Sometimes we chew on & change
our own origins.

Moth: *Christ is the Father,*
        the Son & the Holy Ghost.

                Sani: *Land is Mother & Father is sky.*

Moth: *Moses is the greatest Hoodoo spellcaster.*

                Sani: *A snake created the Amazon River.*

Moth: *A dragon hollowed out the Rhine.*

Sani: *The moon is the eye of a giant owl.*

Moth: *Grandfather always said that*
in the South,
when it's sunny & rains, the devil
is beating
his wife.

Sani: *Touch is like a breeze*
through a shotgun house.

Moth: *The moth is a blessing & an omen.*
The ancestors have your back.

Sani: *Hoodoo reminds me of my beliefs.*

Moth: *It's because the ancestors are important in both.*

Sani: *When it snows,*
the east wind
is starving.

Moth: *Your stomach is growling.*
Are you starving?

Sani: *You make me hungry.*

Moth: *That's good. Don't want to become skin & bones.*

Sani: *I am not so sure.*

"Summer Song" (Moth): *I have found
that the whites of your bones . . .*

"Summer Song" (Sani): *Are so lovely they
should be carved into piano keys.*

SANI NEEDS TO EAT

After driving for a few hours
we rest somewhere in the middle of Virginia.

On the wooden table stained with coffee
the saltshaker is a weight, the creamer the same,
pinning down a map of the United States.

Sani's finger inches along our route & his brows crease.
       Every iota of greenery & pavement we cross
used to be Native land.

My hand wanders over the map,
       sometimes breezing against his.
Taking in the vastness of Sani's truth.
How much is Native land now?

Sani folds his arm in front of him—
       two bricks in a wall I want to hammer down.
According to me? All of it. According to the government,
       something the size of Idaho.

I find Idaho on the map.
Crossed on the table, my arms
       resemble bony brown wings.
If I could fly, I'd pick up the borders of Idaho
       & expand them.

The waiter comes for our order.
I make sure my green dreads cover my face—
I don't like explaining my scar.

Sani orders fluffy towers—pancakes—
& rains them in syrup.

I am not hungry.
        Sani doesn't force me to eat.

I think he knows
freedom has left a hole in my stomach.
I am afraid that if I eat, everything will fall
        through my guts and to the floor.

So I focus on inhaling the essence
of pancakes. Just like the ancestors would
& I am satisfied.

THE ROUTE

My finger travels the course
   marked in red Sharpie,
the paper crisp beneath my finger.

We will grow through
   Virginia
      North Carolina
   Tennessee
Arkansas
   Oklahoma
      Texas & New Mexico.

I wonder if the hole in my stomach will expand
larger with each state
   or fill itself in with something else entirely.

Sani pulls up a list of touristy things on his phone.
   It's not a road trip if we don't explore;
backtrack and get a little lost.

Each pit stop a treasure on the map.

          Is that Sani science?

Sani sticks out his fork, says, *If you eat, will you be nicer?*
            No.

No? Honey? One bite.

*Sani—*I smile—*you just want to eat*
your way across the USA.

I wish I could be that hungry,
but ever since the car split in two
& my stomach sliced open,
my belly cramps on food.

        It forgets to be a stomach.
        It wants to be a storm.

PLACES WE DECIDE TO STOP

1. Monticello Plantation, Charlottesville, Virginia: Where Thomas Jefferson committed several sins; we go to stomp on hateful plantation ground.
2. Natural Bridge, Virginia: A hill holds hands with another hill & we can softly walk across the length of their arms.
3. Ghost Town in the Sky, Maggie Valley, North Carolina: Abandoned amusement park, because each road trip requires an abandoned place where weeds choke everything, where ghosts might linger.
4. Billy Tripp's Mindfield, Brownsville, Tennessee: To see if something beautiful can be made of twisted metal.
5. The Bluebird Cafe, Nashville, Tennessee: Sani likes the food; I like the memories.
6. Fort Smith National Historic Site, Arkansas: Crossroads of the Trail of Tears.
7. Pinnacle Mountain State Park, Arkansas: To swim with the moon.
8. Stafford Air & Space Museum, Weatherford, Oklahoma: To investigate the vastness of the cosmos.
9. The Lighthouse, Palo Duro Canyon State Park, Texas: A rock shaped like a lighthouse; we stand on it with a flashlight & command the sky.
10. Cadillac Ranch, Amarillo, Texas: A photo op with cars.
11. Navajo Nation, Four Corners, New Mexico: Home of the Diné.

MONTICELLO PLANTATION, CHARLOTTESVILLE, VIRGINIA

I snuck
some pancakes
out of the diner in a napkin—
   You have to bring an offering to a plantation.
      For the ancestors.

Thomas Jefferson, a founding father,
   owned one hundred thirty-five bodies.
I add,
   He didn't own
   their souls, though.

The house is round & bald & white
like an eagle's head.

We skip the tour
that builds a toothpick home out of the
goodness in the hearts of plantation owners.

I lead Sani to the back, where the slave quarters
   are left in shambles.
A plaque indicates the location;
   the names of the 135 people are missing.

I don't have a white plate
   like Grandfather taught me.

So I spread the pancakes,
dripping butter & syrup,
on a white napkin & hope
the ancestors will understand.

Now what? Sani sits beside me.
   Now we thank them for their strength & guidance.
I also ask them for joy for Sani, who is always
trying to outrun the shadows around him.

When we open our eyes
   the pancakes are deflated balloons.
That means they took the offering.

Before entering the small graveyard
I tie a scarf around my head.
Grandfather said that would keep
evil spirits from attaching.

Sani & I leave coins
in the small graveyard—
   an offering,
but not nearly enough.
None of this is enough. I frown.

Sani tugs me to him,
places a light-feathered kiss
on the top of my head.

I glance up at him,
          but he is looking
at the death dates on the graves.
He looks down, not at me.
          Through me.
Behind his eyes I see him
building the wall back up.
Death is a strange thing.

I reach for his hand,
          he turns & strides to the car.

I know Sani must be angry—
          with his mother (her silence),
his father (his important work),
his stepfather (his fists),
the universe (for delivering this).

So, even though when he leaves
I feel as empty as a drought
(I can't be mad at him).

The sun is out, so I open my mouth
& imagine devouring it.
I try to fill up on life.

DUST #2

I am sure
at some point a tear
      mixed with soul
escapes my cheek
          & splatters on the ground
               in the tiny graveyard
                    filled with brown bodies.

I hope I do not disturb the dead
        with my molting.

I am stuffed by the sun;
the more I ignite, the more I feel
the heated hands of hell
     reaching up,
        begging me down.
Like now that I am living they remember
they forgot to take me
down
down
down.

THOMAS JEFFERSON HAD
A BLUE BEARD

When I get to the car Sani blinks at me
           & exhales shaky & slow.
On the ride away
           from the place that preserves sin
in spare closets,
I offer Sani the story of the wealthy man,
Bluebeard, who kept murdering his wives
because they broke one rule.

Bluebeard dripped money,
but he was hideous.
           He told his new wife
not to open one door—
just like god told Adam & Eve
not to eat one fruit.
           Being human,
the wife opens the door & finds
the bodies of his other wives,
hanging & bloody.

Most of the founding fathers
           were like that;
they spoke of freedom
but did not offer it to everyone.
They had bodies in their closets.

Sani taps the wheel.

     What's in your closet, Moth?

My hand out the window,

     the breeze

          breaking my fingers.

             Bodies & dirt & metal.

Sani frowns.

     It's not your fault, honey.

I shake my head, loosening the memories of the crash.

     You don't understand—

          I lived too much. I took up too much space.

Sani's jaw works.

     You can't shrink.

          My hands bind together in my lap.

          You shrink, Sani, you try not

          to take up any space at all,

          you don't sing, you don't smile.

Sani white-knuckles the wheel.

Can't you see I am working on that?

          No. I can't.

THINGS I NOTICE ABOUT SANI WHILE HE SINGS "STRANGE FRUIT" BY BILLIE HOLIDAY

1. Two fingers on his right hand bend funny.
2. He sings soft, like he doesn't want to disturb anything living.
3. He feels it all & it is all too much & not enough.
4. He balances thunderclouds on his tongue before swallowing them.
5. He has flown & fallen—like Icarus.
6. That is why he doesn't trust his own wings anymore.

THINGS MY GRANDFATHER
TAUGHT ME ABOUT
THE SOUTH

The enslaved were one-third of the population in the South,
　　　　but their souls were not given any space.

The Constitution licked the lips of slavery
　　　　for more than two hundred years.

Dusty slave quarters with earth for floors
　　　　beside rotundas & white pillars.
Hoodoo was rooted to rebel.
　　　　When the pillars crumbled
America cleared her throat & yelled, *Jim Crow.*

& confederate statues were erected
& loitering became illegal
& prisons became stuffed
with free labor.

& when Black people stepped out of line
they were beaten
& when they stepped out again
photographs were taken of their burning bodies
　　　　& crafted into postcards.

Love notes from the South.
　　　xoxo

THINGS SANI KNOWS
ABOUT THE SOUTH

Everything was green,
      then a white-faced virus
claimed countless souls, clung
to everything, claimed all
the dirt.

Broke the trees,
impaled the land.
Herded humans
away.

Took everything—
      everything,
           everything...
Did not leave a crumb.

NATURAL BRIDGE, VIRGINIA

It looks like the land grew around an ancient giant's head,
        the grass some sort of green crown.
Sani stands in the opening, the breeze
        a wave under his arms. *If this is a giant's head,*
where is the skull?

Dust beneath your feet. I place two coins on the ground—
because lately everywhere I step seems to be a dying place.
A graveyard.

Sani lowers his arms.
        His knees buckle & hit the ground,
his palms cup a handful of dirt
& he chants
a song that hovers in the air.
A song to find the way home,
in case our giant is lost.

We hike to the top. The thick moss impersonates
        dark green hair.

Sani reaches for my hand, as the sun sets.
I say, *I bet our giant*
could cross
the world in one thousand steps.

There is not a soul in sight, but a shadow
                sprouts in front of us, hunchbacked,
long-haired & ancient, slouching westward.
Sani says, *I am trying, Moth.*
I thank the giant for his ancient head
& the perfect view & for helping Sani
want to try to take up more space.

Sani's thumb draws half-moons over my palm
& the shadow shrinks.

Sani whispers
                softer than snow kissing the ground,
                        I don't understand how our thumbprints match.

This time he doesn't pull away.

INTERSTATE 40

After the giant's shadow shrinks into myth
we hike back to the Wrangler & check the map.

Interstate 40 winds from North Carolina & eats up ground
        until it reaches California.

Two thousand five hundred miles
        for the Wrangler to attack.

Sani folds the route back into a rectangle & we climb
        into the Jeep.

He almost smiles & sings:
Stars, fireflies in the sky, flicker on
& the moon
is a hooked fingernail
beckoning us away.

I add it to our "Summer Song."

Moth, tell me a story about the stars.
        Sani hesitates before reaching for my hand,
his thumb on my wrist.

I don't know any stories about stars. I stare straight ahead.

Nighttime is for storytelling.
Sani twines his fingers in mine
like vines growing over my hands.

      Grandfather said nighttime is for the dead.
I follow the lifeline on his palm,
so much longer than my own.

Sani points at the fireflies in the sky.
      The Holy Ones planned the constellations
to help us understand the passage of time.

The Holy Ones placed precious gems on a perfect buckskin—
      the first constellation created was the Big Dipper, or
as we (the Diné) call it, the Male Revolver.

Next more stones were placed on the buckskin
& the Female Revolver (Cassiopeia) was created.

Between them was a fire hearth
      (the North Star)
that kept them warm.

I crane my neck to get a better look at the sky.
      I see them, a man & a woman dancing around Polaris.

Sani's thumb still traces my wrist.

       Would you dance with me in the sky?

No.

       No? The sky is not the ground.
       What if I sing?

It's the ground to someone.
I untwine my fingers from his.

       I can't dance.

       I can't be so ravenous

       when it costs so much.

My heart gallops
when Sani holds my hand.

Speeds too fast,
so I have to let go.

MOTEL #1

1. One bed
2. Mildew & musk & mothballs
3. Twenty bucks
4. Mattress springs that poke
5. Lamp with red fringe
6. *Sani, are you awake?*
7. *Always, honey. Glad you are talking again.*
8. *I thought of a story to tell you.*
9. *A bedtime story, (Moth)?*
10. *It's a long story, (Sani).*
11. *I've got time, (Moth).*
12. *It's a creation story, (Sani).*

OLD SOUTH: PRACTICE APOCALYPSE

Night orbits a house.
It haunts, constricts
until its weight slithers through cracks
& finds an innocent to smother.

Which is fine, because in this story
there are no innocents left.

Sani: *Not one innocent?*
Moth (Me): *Not a single one.*

NEXT

Mama wakes to small handprints fading on the window—
Hercules (the man & the constellation)
is stuck in the cabinet again.

> He rattles & wrestles the dishes like they're hydras.

Sani: *Hydras?*
> Moth (Me): *Really huge snake with infinite heads.*
Sani: *Oh, I see.*

On Sundays, Mama walks to the wooden church—
lets the Holy Ghost hoist her high, throw her down
& play her like a drum.

After church, Mama gathers roots & dirt.
She stuffs every jar in her simple house with blood
& fingernails & shed hair & forget-me-nots
for when the days get long.

Forget-me-nots for when
(Night) wants more than you have to give.

Sani (reaching for my hand): *What does Night want?*
> Moth (Me): *Not much. Night is a sad ghost. She just wants joy.*
Sani (shrugging): *I understand that.*

THEN

The Southern heat causes sweat to fall in tiny drops
around Mama's figure. Mama's black kettle screams of burns.
She paces her nerves by whispering
& having conversations with rusty photographs, ancestors—
old friends.

Sani: *Hold up. Is this a ghost story?*
Moth (Me, standing on the bed, curtsying): *Don't be scared.*

Welcome to the Old South.
Tobacco still in the air,
cotton on the mind.

In the morning, when (Night) leaves
walls return.

From the bay window, cloudy shadows stalk
among the rows of oak trees, one missing a leg,
the other with lashes on its back.

Sani: *Honey, this is definitely a ghost story.*
Moth (Me): *All stories have ghosts.*
Sani (looking sad): *That is true.*

THERE IS MORE

Night is vengeful & brisk—a glass chandelier
in a Southern mansion, beautiful, afraid of heights

but hoisted high.

Sani: *I don't like this story.*
        Moth (Me): *Hush. Almost done.*

One day a rich Black Hoodoo man buys
the weed-laced plantation.
        He has to call on his ancestors to cleanse the home
because the walls shake in protest—
        there is an uprising in the bones of the mansion.

You know, the whip forgets blood,
cotton doesn't recall mahogany hands
        & with all this forgetting, nothing stays.

The Hoodoo man builds a miniature of the plantation,
        takes it down to the river & says,
I will drown you.
        Your shackled hymn, too much glass tearing through skin,
a sound I've been told to put out.

After the Hoodoo man cleanses the plantation, Night leaves,
the ancestors disperse to their favorite rooms.
Behind closed doors a song that sounds like moaning—

Sani (eyebrow raised): *Moaning?*
Moth (smirking): *Moaning.*

The Hoodoo man prepares a feast,
sits at the head of his table,
calls on his ancestors to join.

Ghosts shimmy in with the mosquitoes—
bugs collect, trapped in the net that Pisces has thrown.

By midnight the weed-laced home
at a crossroads is inside out (again)—
& so it goes
&
so it goes.

WE LIE LIKE TWIN SPIRITS

Sani (smiling a real smile):
> *Was that supposed to put me to sleep?*

Moth (Me):
> *I want you*
> > *awake.*
>
> *I don't like closing my eyes.*

Sani (smiling bigger):
> *Look at you taking up space.*
> > *I have a long story to tell you.*

CREATION ACCORDING
TO SANI

The Four Worlds

FIRST WORLD (NI'HODILHIL)
The Diné call it the Black World,
the first peg in a climb to the present,
because there is always a climb.

In the Black World
only Holy People & insects live.

Four columns of clouds
grow from nothing.
Between them First Man
& First Woman
sprout like a miracle
& everything is peace
until it isn't.

The Holy People
set fire to the darkness.
Man & Woman & insects
escape to the Second World
using a big reed.

'Cause sometimes
you just have to run.

Moth (frowning): *Are you always running?*
Me (Sani): *Who isn't?*

SECOND WORLD (NI'HODOOTL'IZH)

It's blue & flows with more life—
   birds, insects & even more Holy People.
First Woman thinks, *Maybe this is home.*
   First Man knows, *There can be many homes.*

They live & live until (again) the Holy People quarrel
& send great winds blowing everything—
First Man & First Woman tumble,
bruised in the Second World.
They can't find a way out.

Then First Man makes a prayer stick
from a reed & carves footsteps
in its flesh. A path appears
& (together) they climb
into the Third World.

Moth (tears in her eyes): *Why are the Holy People mad?*
Me (Sani): *They are not mad. They know of better worlds.*

THIRD WORLD (NI'HALTSOH)

Rivers cut through mountains.
It is bright & yellow & peace-filled.

So peaceful that First Man
& First Woman think,
Maybe we can stay here.

But Coyote (being crafty)
takes Water Monster's baby
& Water Monster
rains & rains in sadness.

The water stretches its fingers
higher & higher.
First Man plants trees,
but none grow tall enough
to escape the flood.

Then he plants a male reed—
it doesn't grow.
Then he plants a female reed—
it stretches to the sky
& they escape to the Glittering World.

Moth: *The female reed grew cause she had to.*
Me (Sani): *She had to save everyone.*

Moth: *Did you need someone to save you, Sani?*
Me (Sani): *I needed someone to see me, Moth.*

FOURTH WORLD (NI'HALGAI)

The Glittering World is where
First Man & First Woman stay.

They plant soil taken from the
Yellow World & grow things.

They find balance.
They live & live
until it is time to die
peacefully.

Moth: *Maybe they don't have to die.*
Me (Sani): *Everyone has a death date, Moth.*

Moth: *Maybe they turn into mermaids*
                    in the Third World & hide & live & live.
Me (Sani): *I'll hide with you in any world you want, Moth.*

WE SLEEP

Eventually my eyes do close,
my head tucked under Sani's chin,
my hands fast around his shirt,
his hands on my back, holding me
        close & closer & closest.

        Our "Summer Song"
        is a red string lacing
        our tendons together.

        When I smile, he smiles.
        When he frowns, I frown.

        It happens naturally, like magic.

There is not a particle between us.
Like we are buried in the same hole.

ON OUR WAY
TO NORTH CAROLINA

Sani sings
      loud, with a smile
that fits around the sadness in his face
over & over again.

Honey, all the clocks are against us,
      we've got one summer, I'll do your bidding.
Just tell me what you want.
I'll do anything you want.

GHOST TOWN IN THE SKY, MAGGIE VALLEY, NORTH CAROLINA

On nights we sleep close & unseam in the morning,
the places where we no longer touch feel raw.

We follow Rich Cove Road almost four thousand feet up
       into the sky. So high up, I think if it were dark
I might be able to taste stars.

The amusement park in the sky is closed
& abandoned, but on road trips
       you shatter rules, so we sneak in.

The grass has taken back most of the rides.
I sit on a railing looking out at the mountains
we drove through.

Something metal falls & I jump.
Sani still watches the trees.

Sani says: *My people think ghosts are tricksters.*

       What's wrong with a trick? (I ask.)

       Sani says: *Sometimes tricks hurt your heart.*
              My people think ghosts can cling tightly to you.

Like a shadow suit?

Sani's frown lines collect like a crash: *Yes.*

& he digs into his pockets,
pulls out the pills wrapped in cloth.
They are clear & stuffed
with dried plants.
        Pops two orbs (filled with herbs) into his mouth
& slices through the weeds, away from me.

HOLDING MY BREATH

I inhale deep.
Sani doesn't reach for my hand;
   he drives with his jaw screwed shut,
     with knuckles white.

I wonder if he feels it, too,
like nothing will be close enough
so maybe far away is better.

The feeling when we fell asleep,
tucked together like twin ghost stories in a book—
our skin reached out & grew together.

It is scary to think of ripping apart each morning,
   so scary,
I forget to exhale.

I imagine smoothing
Sani's creased brow
& he looks at me, startled.

How strange,
how quickly lifelines merge
like the vines in me
reach across air to
play in his hair.

SUNRISE INN MOTEL

Sani looks at me again, but he still won't talk.

There is only one bed, again;
this time we split it
      with a fault line of feathered pillows.

I stretch my legs, weary from ten hours in the car.
      Sani turns off the light & even though we don't touch,
we share the darkness that pushes into each of us.

I am grateful that in the morning
my skin won't have to rip from his.

Sani turns to me. *It hurts to know you will leave.*
      It's hard. Everything leaves me.
        My voice, my heart, my mom.

        Your voice won't leave you.
        I won't leave, Sani.

You will.

        I won't.

Honey, you will.

      He says it like a prophecy
      I can't rewrite.
      But your voice won't.

BILLY TRIPP'S MINDFIELD, BROWNSVILLE, TENNESSEE

When Sani looks at art he inspects it like a thing
        you love without knowing why.

Sometimes Sani looks at me like I am the Glittering World.

Sometimes he looks through me
like I am wispy fog.

Today he looks at me,
        in me,
eyes shaded as I swing on the twisted metal,
taking up all the space I can
while there is still time.
Swinging wildly by the hotel,
where we split everything in two
so we would not have to *feel* anything.

It's the largest outdoor sculpture in Tennessee.
        Some parts are so tall, they threaten to
puncture the sun.

I swing & Sani asks me, *But how far down in the ground*
        do you think the metal goes?
                I smile into the sun. *It grows from hell;*
                  these are the horns of the devil.

Swinging feels like dancing but not exactly.
Swinging reminds me of being a kid.
Reminds me of when my hands were so small
that when Dad and I crossed the street
on our way to the local playground
he would only put out his middle & pointer fingers
for my tiny hand to grasp.

I smile & a smile opens Sani's lips & shows his teeth,
a smile just for me. He asks,

> *How did you become home so quickly?*

I swing again.

> *Magic, Sani. Magic.*

HOME

It is strange that each town we inch through,
with its estimated population, is someone's *home*.

A place that is so much a part of their bones,
they can't *home* anything else.

His (Sani's) favorite "Summer Song" lyric so far:
I want to suffocate your sadness.

My (Moth's) favorite "Summer Song" lyric so far:
I have found that the whites of your bones are so lovely,
they should be carved into piano keys.

I'd say this Wrangler
is the first *home* I can recall in two years.

Sani says: *I don't think it's my fault*
my stepfather hates me.
I don't think Mom knows
how to leave anyone again.

Moth: *It's not your fault, Sani.*
Grandfather says
some people are just born unbalanced.
They are just born hateful.

THE BLUEBIRD CAFE,
NASHVILLE, TENNESSEE

I have been here once before.
For dinner
      after a national dance competition.

Three years ago,
      Mom sat at the table by the window,
her hair slick in a severe high bun.

My nails drag across my palms,
      trying to extend the lifelines
of everyone I love.

I sip from Sani's drink.
      It tastes like dust & it tastes like blood.
The glass shatters in my hand.

Sani puts money on the table.

Sani touches my arm,
      leads me away
      from the window
      & out the door.

He pulls me into the car,
        holds me together
like he knows
I might spill out through my scar.

But it's not enough,
the heated hands of hell
are coming for me—
I was supposed to die with them
in the car that split
        like a candy bar.

My body slipping away from itself,
so I open the door.
        I run
                I run
                        I run away.
Without Sani,
just like he told me I would.

DUST #3

I am sure
      some of me fell
           through my scar
                onto the table
of the Bluebird Cafe.
      I am sure
           it has already been swept up.
                So I can never get it back—
                    I don't think.
                Look at me, leaving myself places.
                Living so lofty, so *dusty*—
                taking up so much space.

MOTEL WHATEVER

I find my way back
        to the motel
& find Sani making a rocking chair
of his body.

Knees tucked to his chin, swaying
        back & forth
until I appear in front of him
        & he reaches for me,
        tucks me under his chin.
He smooths his hands
        over my back.

I rest here, cocooned
        & harden for hours.

Sani says, *I don't know how to*
        be whole anymore.

I say, *Whatever you need*
you can borrow from me.

Sani convinces me
        that if I stand on his feet & sway,
it is not the same as dancing.
I say I will if he sings.

His voice vibrates the vines in me.
My tiny feet on his & he holds
my waist & he sways like I weigh nothing.

I close my eyes,
try to hold it together
            as I remember what dance feels like—

for a moment I am full
                        on movement.

WILLOW: NASHVILLE CEMETERY

We make an unplanned stop
because, according to Sani,
we've got time & that is what you do
on road trips.

The sun sets over our Wrangler outside the cemetery
my grandfather brought me to ten years ago.

I drop coins by the entrance,
by the wrought iron gate with pointy tips
like iron teeth.

We find the spot where my gray-bearded grandfather opened
the ground beneath a willow, at the crossroads.

Where he chanted to the spirits—thanking them
for their wisdom
& knowledge as he poured whiskey into the dry hole he created.

I wonder if he knew
that our car would split in two
& our family would split in two
& my face would split in two.

We dig & dig,
find the photo of my grandfather
& me, hands linked

like chains in a fence,
but both our faces are rotted away—

                              gone.

The feather is
        still as crisp
                as the day it was buried.

Sani smells the feather.
        It smells like mountain smoke. It looks familiar.
                        Still smells like mountain smoke?
I frown.
Still, he whispers, cradling the feather to his heart.

        Sani hands me the feather like he is handing me his soul.
Your grandfather was a great Hoodoo man, Moth.

I exhale the smell of smoke. *But even the greatest*
        Hoodoo man can't bring back the dead.

I dig deeper in the hole
& pull out an envelope.
Inside is a dusty,
musty Juilliard application.
Looks like it was printed out
a decade ago.

Sani exhales,
pulls out his mystery pills
cradled in fabric, filled with dried plants
& a cloud covers his face.

BRUISES

Sani is silent as we ride
the vine of the road to our next motel.

His sadness comes in waves
            & sometimes, if the moon
is high enough in the sky,
secrets tsunami out of him
& crash into the air.

Secrets like:
            My mom went to college in New Mexico,
far away from her father's bruising hands
& she met my dad (gentle & healing).

Things like:
            Father was busy healing,
                        Mother was busy packing.
Kindness could not keep her.
I felt like an accident
tossed from nation (Navajo) to nation (United States).

Secrets like:
            Father said that on the day I was born
                    I cried so hard, it started raining—
I held sadness closer than my own ghost.
It's always been like that;
I've always needed pills,

blue-and-white pills,
but I need them less with you.

I notice the things Sani doesn't say—
like how the bruise around his eye
changes from blue to brown
& now it is faint but yellow & orange.

Not yellow like
the color of the golden sun.
More like the color
of actual gold
tucked into the dirt,
hiding—
in Sani's skin.

MOTEL GUITAR LESSONS

Sani is teaching me to play guitar
      in a random motel
      because I told him my brother
      was going to teach me
      before we broke in half.

Outside the rain tap-dances;
      inside it is humid & the air conditioner
wants to be an off-key saxophone.

It is too hot, but still Sani pulls me onto his lap
      & places the guitar in front of us.

He teaches me three different chords,
      showing my fingers where to press.
I've missed playing. He smiles. *I forgot how much*
      I've missed this.

He rests his chin on my shoulder,
      whispering, *Good job, honey,*
even when I mess up.

I lean back into him,
tracing the tattoos on his skin.
      Voltage on our tongues,
glows ballerina-witchcraft.

Sani leans into my ear,
his breath kissing
my green hair.

   Honey, your hands are fluent
in foreplay, all curves & a little bite.

My fingers lace into his.
   This is going to be a long song.

His lips breeze
against the soft skin behind my ear.
   Maybe it's a song
     that never has to end . . .
      maybe . . .

TIME IS NOTHING BUT
AN ILLUSION

Tucked in beside Sani I say,
Did you know one day on Venus
            is equal to two hundred forty-three days on Earth?

                        Sani watches my mouth as I speak.
                            That explains it, then.
                            We are living on Venus time.

I nod:
            I've known you for seven years.
I nuzzle even closer,
my lips graze his neck
& his heart beats
so recklessly in his chest,
I think it might explode.

FORT SMITH NATIONAL
HISTORIC SITE, ARKANSAS

Sani wants me to see Fort Smith.

        He says, *My dad brought me here when I was young.*

There is information about the fort

written on wooden plaques covered in glass.

        It says where the gallows were,

its foundation sticking up from the dirt

like a stony hand.

I don't have enough coins to place here,

at a crossroads of the Trail of Tears.

Sani touches the cool ground, his eyes

dart over the landscape, he shakes his head—

        So many ghosts linger here, so much pain.

My fingers curl over his shoulder.

Sani's hand covers mine. *The Cherokee lost*

        one-quarter of their population. That's what the sign says,

they lost their way of life, their Motherland.

Sani grinds his teeth: *Father taught me that there are five hundred*

sixty-eight Native American tribes

        but only three hundred twenty-six reservations.

There are many forts with plaques thanking settlers
         for pushing west, for goldrushing & eating the land.

Sani traces the plaque.
         I guess land only belongs to white faces.

I do the only thing I can do.
Listen.

TIME TRAVEL MOTEL

It's raining tap dancers again
& the motel is dim
& Sani can't sleep
after going to the fort, so
   I offer him a story
to hush
    hush his mind.

I hush
the pain ricocheting
in his skull. I tell him how to adore
the moon so much you can taste it—
like lemon-spun cotton candy.

I offer him another story
where I change time
   & become a giant
     & move the car that split mine in two
like a tiny chess piece in my fingers. I tell him
that he can meet my brother, mother & father.

Sani folds in. *You can't do that, honey.*
   You can't be the giant who moves the car
   & be in the car at the same time.

      I can, it's my story.
    In my bones I know he is right
     & that makes me ache.

I stand up & head to the door.
I need space to fly, to escape,
but Sani appears in front of me,
eyes bright.

Please don't leave. Not yet.
Everything is too loud without you.

I can be the giant & in the car!
I think I am yelling.

I am sorry. So sorry, but you can't.
That's not how it works.

I remind him, crying, of our "Summer Song":
Just tell me what you want.
I'll do anything you want.

Sani stops.
Frowns. Runs to the closet
& pulls out an iron.

How about an iron to smooth the creases
that wrinkle up your spirit?

I laugh (I can't help it).
Sani laughs ('cause I laugh).
We are both laughing
so hard
we cry
& cry
& feel
& live.

MOTEL MORNING RITUALS
(WITH SANI)

I always wake before him
            & untangle from his embrace.
I tuck his hair behind his ear
& kiss his forehead
before gathering
the box of roots
Grandfather gave me.

I use the TV stand
as an altar & Sani always remembers
to leave food wrapped in a white napkin
from the night before in the fridge
for an offering.

I pray to the ancestors
(mostly to Grandfather),
thanking them for the boy
with waterfall hair.

Sometimes Sani's eyes
stay closed & sometimes
they flutter open & he groans,
crawling across the floor
to kneel beside me.

Sani (looking sad): *Do the ancestors ever answer?*

Me (Moth): *They sent me you.*

PINNACLE MOUNTAIN STATE PARK, ARKANSAS

Eventually the rain eases up on its reins.
The sky still seems angry, but we drive anyway.
         We eat up more road until we can see
Pinnacle Mountain, which stretches itself
         slowly toward the sky.
I want to climb it & meet heaven
         because I think that is where Mom & Dad
             & brother & Grandfather are.

Sani lifts his arms above his head, making a mountain
         with his hands & it starts to rain (again).
It is like only the water & wind live here.

I feel filled, like a caterpillar gorged;
my clothes are too tight,
my body too small,
so I lift my top over my head.

Next my jeans melt from my legs.
I jump into the lake.
         Sani follows, revealing more tattoos
than I could have guessed.

The sky & the rain baptize our bodies—
         sinless & free.

We could live here, he says,

    black hair hiding his eyes.

                    Why just live?

                I disappear under the water,

                    for a moment

              existing somewhere else.

You remind me, he says almost to himself,

    how nice sound can taste.

                  We could thrive here.

IT FEELS LIKE
THE SECOND WORLD

Floating naked & weightless,
joined by the tips
of our feathered fingers,
we are all water;
we take up 70 percent
of the earth.

Sani tells me
of the Second World again:

Filled with birds
         lighter than air
                  weightless for twenty-three days

until the world grew heavy

& First Man
& First Woman
are pushed to the Third World.

STORYTELLING

Sani turns away from me
      as I pull layers of clothes
           on, strapping myself
back into the mundane.

I accidently peek & see another
      tattoo of five finger grass
on his back & I worry who
      (other than me)
wants him to do their bidding.

The car ride is silent as our headlights
      somehow lead us miles
while only letting us see twenty feet at a time.

Moths misunderstand the Wrangler's orb eyes.
I find myself flinching
as each one hits.

Sani is unfazed
by the cemetery on the car windshield.
& (again) I wonder if he is the moon
or a lightbulb.

CAR RIDE: STORYTELLING

Sani:
You tell stories
the same way
I think you would dance.
> *Sure & full & alive,*
>> *alive.*

Moth:
> *You sing*
>> *like an oak tree.*
>> *Slow & strong & measured.*

Sani:
Moth, I want you so close,
I can feel your laugh
before it comes . . .
> *but this is hard.*

Moth:
> *Because we are both a little chipped,*
>> *like old china?*

Sani:
I am chipped china,
you're a kaleidoscope—
> *pieces always shifting & growing.*

Moth:
Shifting?
Away from you?
You still think I'll leave.

Sani:
Honey, I want you so close,
            but I don't know if it's possible.

Moth:
Because I am impossible?

Sani:
You are certainly something
entirely your own.

Moth:
What are you?

Sani:
A broken voice.
What are you?

Moth:
Oh, I am the smoke
            & the fire.

Sani:
& the wave
& the lighthouse
& the match—
you set everything ablaze.

STAFFORD AIR & SPACE MUSEUM, WEATHERFORD, OKLAHOMA

According to science, the universe exploded
      & has been expanding ever since.

Trillions of light-years across
      & one day we will all just freeze because
there won't be enough suns to heat us.

According to Sani, there are four worlds
& in every one I might leave him
like everyone leaves him.
In every one his mind is a cluttered attic
with tiny clouds constantly storming
& his pills sometimes help the sun poke through.

According to the Bible, Adam & Eve
are kicked out of Eden.
      In Sani's story, humanity is pushed
out of three worlds before they find home.

According to god, it only took seven days
to craft
      reality
& according to my grandfather, the ancestors linger
close; if you listen, they can tell you the truth of all of it.

I've been listening & I don't hear anything—
       the ancestors close their lips to me.

Every story
       as impossible
              as the next.
                     All true.

According to me, *temptation* is a sin
       that Jesus forgot to write down.

I want the universe
to stop tempting me
with so much life—
then pulling back.

I am not sure I can take
       the stretch
& pull of it anymore.

THE LIGHTHOUSE, PALO DURO CANYON STATE PARK, TEXAS

There is a rock called the Lighthouse
            where, for a moment, the ground doesn't know
it is the ground—it could be some dusty-colored ocean.

The rock doesn't know it is a symbol.
            The stars, staggered & graveyarding,
don't know they are constellations.

Sani winks. *How do we know we are alive?*
            I shrug. *Because we can feel the wind.*

Sani salutes the Lighthouse. *So that's all, we just have*
            to keep feeling?

I push my locs out of my face.
            Feeling & believing.

Sani stands so close.
            I want to believe, I want to feel.

He stands so close,
I can *feel* his heartbeat through the air.
            I'll help you feel, Sani. I'll help you believe.

Moth's favorite "Summer Song" lyric so far:

> *Honey, all the clocks are against us.*

Sani's favorite "Summer Song" lyric so far:

> *Honey, all the clocks are against us.*

CADILLAC RANCH,
AMARILLO, TEXAS

Sani has me stand in the picture.
He sketches the cars & the peaks, hands it to me & says,

You blend in.

DREAM LOVE: MOTEL

The column of his spine is taller when
traced,
laced with black
& gray tattoos.

His hands
on my hands,
my eyes,
my
everywhere.

I feel alive.
Alive. Alive.

Sani kissing a green moth
out of his mouth
& another
& he is choking.

I wake up
staring at Sani.

Sani sleeps,
breathing heavier than usual.

                      Clothed.

                              But dreaming of hands

                                    everywhere,

            everywhere.

LUNA MOTH

It's larger than
the width
of a throat.

      Dripping green paint with illusion eyes.
It *knows* it is the prettiest.

It is even given the moon's name.

Strangely, it is still tricked
by artificial light.

This should (also) be a sin—
      but I wish I could just know things
            without a trace of doubt.

Like the planted seed knows to grow
& the sun knows to burn
& my legs know to dance
& Sani's voice knows it should
sing
      sing
           sing.

NAVAJO NATION,
FOUR CORNERS, NEW MEXICO

It's the size of West Virginia.

> Which is far too small . . . to be fair
> in any & every story.

COCOON:

a) a shell a caterpillar creates
b) the first magic trick
c) another boundary

(Moth) You will know your story all at once
or not at all.

> —Gray-Bearded Grandfather
> (Rootworker)

FOUR CORNERS

Arizona, Colorado, New Mexico & Utah

The only place in the United States
      where four state lines kiss.
Like four barefoot girls
holding hands & circling
a campfire.

This entire region is a crossroads
dripping with magic—
      the sandy dirt so vibrant with spirits,
it glitters in the sun.

It feels like the ground reaches
up to cradle the wheels of our car—
I think we might be flying.

The land remembers Sani,
      Sani remembers the land.
            Because the land is me, Moth.

He is right; the breeze
sings through the car
& plays with my hair.

COCOON

When a caterpillar is stuffed, it hardens again.
      The intentional shell.

Sani & I arrive at the reservation.

      He says, *I can feel the Motherland cradling me.*

I feel safe in this car, this desert of glittering dirt
      with sleeping bags in the back seat & the road ahead.

Sani says, *I would like to direct the stars.*

Which I think means,
      anything is possible.

I think he is right.
I have not thought of my scar, like the tip of a whip.
I have not slathered Vaseline on it to make it glisten less true.

I have not crammed
my spirit too small
to fit in a space
smaller than my pinky's tip
in days
& days.

The Motherland feels different than my egg of a room
        at Aunt Jack's, my egg of a life in Virginia.

I don't even mind that she has not called,
not even once.

I'll rest here,
caged on this holy land
& grow.

When it is time to uncage,
I don't mind if the cocoon is dropped
& I splatter like a Pollock painting—
a little bruised but
free
free
free
& flying.

WE FOLD DOWN THE SEATS
& SLEEP IN THE BACK
OF THE JEEP

With the trunk open,
sharing one sleeping bag.

The right angle of Sani's arm
has been my pillow for many days.

When I fall asleep
I dream the same dream,
especially when Sani & I sleep
back to back,
conjoined at our spines.

I dream red lines—
guitar strings strumming music
crisscross our bodies, binding us tight.

I dream that on this land older than myth
some sort of magic communes between us.

I ALSO DREAM

Grandfather is waving to me
in a cemetery I don't know.
      & Sani is beside him,
young, only coming to his hip.
His eyes are a crowded attic
of ghosts & hurt.

Grandfather pats Sani's head
      & hands him the five finger grass.

In my dream Sani eats the grass
& coughs up a white feather
he hands to Grandfather.

In my dream Sani stretches tall
      in the span of a second
& the five finger grass he swallowed
appears as tattoos on his skin.

I wake up panicked.
      Sani is still asleep & I trace
his tattoos, trying to translate
the untranslatable.

CAR RIDE TO WINDOW ROCK

Moth (application on phone): *It doesn't hurt
to apply to Juilliard, Sani.*

Sani (driving): *I won't get in.*

Moth (annoyed): *Yeah, you won't
if you don't apply.*

Sani (pulling over): *Moth, singing is sometimes
too much truth.*

Moth (voice shaking): *But when you sing,
Sani, the universe startles & listens.
Your soul is lighter after—like it can fly.*

Sani (car parked, facing me): *I've fallen
too many times, Moth.*

Moth (voice soft): *You're no Icarus;
you can write a new origin story
with your violin voice.*

Sani (serious): *Honey, my mind
has locked
my violin voice away.*

Moth (smirking): *I hid the key*
in my mouth.

Sani (very serious): *Would you like me to find it?*

Moth (nodding): *Your future*
depends on it.

KISSING SANI (FEELS LIKE . . .)

Witnessing a blue sunset on Mars;
     harvesting the notes that are impossible to sing.

As natural as the gray wolf
moving the moon across the sky
     without misplacing her howl.

Like keeping company with the mouths of mermaids;
     a sea burial—benthic creatures peacefully encroaching.

It's like if a blue whale lost its soul mate for a decade,
then when they find each other
they sing
& dance
& the ocean tsunamis with them, saying:
Look at that,
     their tongue prints still match.

Like home
     home
          home.

WINDOW ROCK

It's the capital of the Navajo Nation
& looks like cookie dough
      with a space taken out
by a perfect circle cookie cutter.

Sani says, *Ni' Ałníi'gi, which means "Center of the World"*—
      its first name.
A long time ago
there used to be water here
& medicine men would travel here
from very far with woven jugs
      to collect water for Blessingway ceremonies.

I stare up at it.
A larger
      miracle
the longer I watch it.

ALMOST AT SANI'S HOUSE & MOTHS PEPPER THE WINDSHIELD

Moth: *There are more than one hundred sixty thousand species of moths.*
The black witch moth can migrate long distances.

> Sani: *I migrate*
> *from the Motherland to Virginia.*
> *So I'll be that one.*

Nobody wants to be the common clothes moth;
         its gluttony is legendary. The peppered moth's wings
are sprinkled with dark splatters on a tan canvas.

The atlas moth is one of the largest,
but, as a sacrifice, it has no mouth—
         it doesn't eat from birth to death.
The hummingbird moth predates the hummingbird.

The luna moth, greenish yellow & grand, is the priest—
it holds communion at its altar. The other moths
sometimes confuse it for the moon.

Moth: *Which moth should I be?*

Sani (jaw working): *As a caterpillar,*
the sphinx moth
entombs itself an inch in the soil
before it flies home.

Moth: *Hoodoo work?*
I'll take that,
I'll be magic & mystery.

SANI'S HOME

The house is small & filled with food.
      A worn-out La-Z-Boy rocks
in front of a tiny TV with foil on the antennas.
It reminds me of a moth's bushy feelers.

All Sani's father says to him is
      Your hair looks shorter, but your eyes
seem brighter, that's good
before he leaves through the front door
      without saying hello to me.

I wonder how his father can tell,
      when Sani's hair is always tied tight
in a bun. I guess fathers just know
these things.

He is like that before he goes to heal people.
      Sani squeezes my hand.
Makes me think of my aunt (Jack)
      always maneuvering around me,
worried my shrinking might shrink her.

I bet it takes a lot of energy to heal,
      I say, thinking of my scar.

HOW TO MAKE PB&J
ACCORDING TO SANI

1. Two slices of bread
2. Peanut butter & jelly
3. Peanut butter first, on both bread slices
4. Jelly next, on one bread slice
5. Only one scoop
6. Sani says, *Peanut butter on both slices is important.*
7. I (Moth) say, *To keep them from blending together.*

SANI'S ROOM

One twin bed.

    One lamp.

        One dresser.

           & a large map.

His dresser has sketches

    of birds & mountains

        & a girl with black & gray moths for hair

           with a scar down her face

                like the tip of the whip.

I grab the picture. *When did you draw this?*

                            Years ago. He shrugs.

The girl is dancing in it.

                                 Yes.

That's strange.

                             A little.

Is it me? I swallow.

                 At first Sani doesn't answer.

                 Instead he pulls the feather

           we found in the graveyard ground

                     from his backpack

                  & places it on his dresser.

I find the picture
of Grandfather & me.
I put it on top of the feather
because they seem to go together.

I've dreamed of your face before,
but your hair was a swarm
of fluttering moths.

"SAMSON," A SONG BY REGINA SPEKTOR

It's one of Sani's favorite songs.
        He plays it
when he threatens to cut his hair. Which would be a shame
        but seems to be the opposite of what his father wants.
So he might.

I think it will be hard for him. I think about cutting
it for him, in his sleep & maybe he will wake up not even noticing.

Maybe his father could blame me & not Sani.
        His father left again without a word—
        he just put a cloth filled with those mystery pills
        on the kitchen counter and left
            carrying so much weight on his shoulders.

Why is it always like this?
The ones who are hard as stone,
the ones who don't expand
& contract like a pupil
exposed to light,
are left to crack slowly.

If Sani were more cave than stone,
        I'd crawl into him. To prove I would not leave.
To prove he can carry something so alive.

In the end,
Sani keeps his hair because some things aren't worth
            waking up weaker.

Sani reaches for the cloth
filled with mystery pills
on the kitchen counter.
I think he might take one (again),
maybe they help like when he takes
his white-and-blue ones (consistently)
so that his sadness comes in steady waves
instead of a spiraling typhoon.
He doesn't open the cloth; he throws it in the trash can
            & pulls me close, forehead to forehead—
            Maybe you won't leave.
                        Maybe. Maybe. You can haunt my dreams.

I whisper a new "Summer Song" lyric:
Honey, you can keep me forever,

                        like a phantom limb.

SANI'S DAD IS A
MEDICINE MAN

He can heal the hurt in anything & I wish
I knew a language to make him look right at me,
to make him understand
that my hurt is farther down.

Not even in me.
Maybe in the ground around me.
Rooted.

Sani's dad does tell us a story on our third night,
          about the man dressed as a wolf. The dead man.

About not grieving at a grave for too long
because the spirit might stay & become a trickster.

He says, *You should fear ghosts,* but I would take my family
see-through, like *papier-mâché,* or solid.

Sani says, *What's wrong with remembering too much?*
          His father crosses his weathered arms. *You forget*
why the breeze is a miracle & why the stars are a gift.

SANI'S NIGHTMARES

Sani is screaming
in his sleep,
clawing
at his skin
like the heated
hands of hell
are coming for him.

He can't sing
between sobs,
so even though
my voice is dusty,
I sing as best I can
to him—
       & eventually he sleeps.

SANI'S DAD REFILLS HIS MYSTERY PILLS

& Sani plops the clear orbs
into his mouth (again).

Every day, twice a day,
for many days.

I don't know what they do—& Sani won't tell me—
        but they make him different.
Harder to touch, but his mind
seems less attic-with-ghost—
more attic-of-blankness.

I don't mind;
at least when Sani dreams,
he doesn't scream.

HEALTH SYSTEM

　　　　Sani is sick
& it is not something his father's (mystery pills)
can heal; sadness still wears Sani like a suit.

In Navajo medicine there are steps
in the healing process
　　　　& a different medicine man dedicated to each step.

One medicine man smokes out the problem.
Herbs are prescribed by another.
　　　　A mixture is made by another.

Sani has been through this process many times—
　　　　taken herbs & Western pills.

His soul is still sometimes broken-feeling—
less when he sings, more on his Motherland.

Sani doesn't tell me that part.
That is what I hear his father saying:
You know you have to take both of your pills
this close to your ancestors.
You have to be consistent with them,
not just here & there—that's not
how it works.

His father says that to him
over & over again,
each time Sani thinks about
flushing the (mystery)
pills down the toilet.
Over & over again Sani says,
I know, I know,
but when I am consistent
I can't see the truth
clearly. Even the moon
seems different.

& the nightmares always follow.
His father keeps refilling the cloth
sitting open on the kitchen counter
& I keep offering as much life as I can spare.

WE HAVE COCOONED HERE

One day after flushing the pills down the toilet,
Sani looks at me, not sort of through me.

He says, *We have been in the Motherland for two weeks.*

Which, to me, somehow
         only feels like two days,
but to Sani feels like Venus time.

It is as if part of me has slept;
I drift through days
& skip through weeks
like skipping stones
over water.

COYOTE STORY: FIRST SCOLDER

Because Sani's dad won't talk to me,
we go camping. On the ride to the site
a coyote crosses our path.

> Sani leans in & grabs my hand.
> *We have a lot of stories about the coyote.*

I draw circles on Sani's palm.
Tell me a story, Sani.

> Sani brings my fingers to his mouth & kisses them:
> *Coyote is mischievous in the Third World.*
> *In the Third World there are animals*
> *in abundance. Coyote steals Water Buffalo's children.*
> *In anger Water Buffalo calls a flood,*
> *which forces the First Man & First Woman to leave*
> *the Third World & go to the Fourth.*

I remember that story, I say.

> Sani's grip tightens around my hand.
> *There are also skinwalkers.*
> *Evil things that lurk around*
> *at night. Do you want*
> *to go back?*

We don't turn back.
We drive faster.

BLOOD MOON IN NEW MEXICO

By the time we reach the campsite
the moon is as old & golden as captured fireflies.
     We open the back of the Wrangler & spread a blanket.

          Sani: *Tilting the light, Coyote is many things. Like a soul.*

Moth: *Souls love chaos, I suppose.*
Moth: *How come you don't talk to many people here?*

                    Sani: *You talk to me, honey.*
Moth: *Answer the question.*
                    Sani: *They think my mind is cursed.*

Moth: *Is it?*

                    Sani: *I used to think so.*
                    Now I don't know the difference
                    between a miracle & a curse.

FIRESIDE CHAT

Sani: *If you could do anything, what would you do?*

Moth: *I would dance with the soil, every moment—*
everything would be my soundtrack.
Cicada hymns & basketball thuds.
I'd go to Juilliard & dance in everyone's
minds & live forever.

Silence. Chirping.

Moth: *If you could do anything, what would you do?*

Sani: *I'd write songs.*
Slow ones, sad ones, soft ones
sealed with small kisses for you.
I'd play my guitar on corners,
then on stages, then in stadiums.
I'd grow & live & live
onstage every night.

Silence.

Moth: *Why can't we do that?*

Sani: *Because you won't dance*
& I hardly sing or play
& everyone says I can't.

Moth: *If you play & sing, I'll dance.*

GUITAR & VOICE & DANCE

Sani's fingers have scars
on their tips
from plucking strings.

His voice rides the wind,
ignites my spine,
sets my toes on fire.

He wants to write songs;
he wants to write things
so big they stretch from
the Navajo Nation
around the equator
& back.

He used to play all the time;
he used to sing all the time.

Before his dad got busy
& his mom got lonely & left
& his mind kept poking itself
& his stepfather kept sticking him.

But tonight he plays
& sings
& I spill alive, dancing.

DANCING

Dancing again feels like glass feathers
falling on a silver city.

Like Grandfather coaxing magic
from roots.

Like god is in the brown dirt
I stomp on.

Sani keeps singing
& I keep dancing—with a hint of *swallow your pills,*
            wash it back with bathtub moonshine,
which of course also feels like the color of dusty
Carolina heat & humid New York summers
& riding bikes with no training wheels.

I dance
like the west wind
is winding,
twining
our souls together
like red strings.

WHEN THE SONG IS OVER

I am weightless.
Sani is breathless.
His mouth finds mine.

PUZZLE IN THE SKY

Sani: *The stars are a puzzle of myths.*
'Cause we all look up, we can't help it.

Moth: *Will you keep singing?*
Will you keep taking your blue-&-white pills?
Will you keep taking the clear orb pills
your father leaves on the kitchen counter?

Sani: *I don't know if the price*
of getting better is
worth it.

Moth: *Life, a chance on a stage,*
       even if only for two seconds,
              is worth every pill—every scarred finger.

Sani: *Will you keep dancing?*

Moth: *That's different. I am guilty.*

Sani: *No, honey, you're innocent.*

Moth: *Sani . . . there are no more innocents left.*

Sani: *Moth,*

        you

            are

                innocent.

SANI'S NOTE

"Where I Want to Go," a Song by Roo Panes

I dedicate
this song to you.

I can't get
the words right
& I know
if you really
knew me,
thought my thoughts,
you would not
want me.

I can't have you.
You're not someone I can hold.

Even though I was
a beach with no sand,
a starless sky before you.

What am I
when you leave?
Maybe it is better
just to leave now.

If we could stay
in this cocoon,
if we could stay,
if we could stay
in this Fifth World
we created with stories
& song lyrics
& dance.

I dream
about you
all the time.

Of my hands learning
the topography of you.

But dreamers wake,
fables end, lyrics are forgotten
& cocoons break
open, eventually.

DISASSEMBLE

Sani leaves me at the campsite
        with a note that feels like a forever goodbye.
He leaves me with food, water & the Wrangler
with its keys.

It is like he is asking me to leave—
        begging me to go.

For the first time in a long time
I feel the heated hands of hell
reaching through the ground.

I pull out Aunt Jack's iPhone
& google *humanity*.

There is a Walmart only a mile away.
It helps to know there are lights
& noise close by, it makes me feel alive

                              alive.

My scar aches & wants to burst open.
        I tuck my knees to my chin.

I won't do it,
            I won't trust Sani with his lava hair,
campfire eyes & five finger grass tattoo
            ever again.
                        He has to be doing
someone else's bidding.
I danced
& he left,
just like
everyone else.

ALONE

I don't know if Sani has been gone
for a day or two or three.

I have forgotten to count the moons
& I sleep in the car
& only think of the graveyard
of stars.

I think tomorrow is the day.

I'll walk away,
to the Walmart.
Disappear.

NOTE LEFT IN SANI'S CAR

"All My Life," a Song by Texada

I dedicate
this song
to you.

I was
the sticky filling
that survived
the crash
because I had to live
for this.

I think
there might have been
a line fating us to meet.

I think it was buried
red & bright in the earth,
strung from the Motherland
to the candy bar car.

It yanked me
hard enough
to fracture.

Soft enough
to make sure
I crossed your path.

Do you think
there is still a string
underground
connecting us?

When the car
crashed, did you feel
me shatter?

When you close
your eyes & play
& sing, do you feel
me dancing?

If I melt away,
reassemble wrong,
will you find me?

I am leaving.
It might be best.

Just promise me you'll audition
& take your pills
& live, live, live.

HOW OUR WORLD WAS CREATED

I am halfway to Walmart,
tears making riverbeds
of my cheeks.

I am ready to disappear
when I hear Sani yelling
from the Wrangler.

I keep walking
          on the side of the road.

He yells again, begs me to stop.

I keep walking.

He pulls off the road,
jumps out of the truck
& stands in front of me,
a cigarette dangling
between his soft lips.

I pause
          & pause.

Sani has dark circles under his eyes.

I wish I could scrub them away with my sleeve
like I scrubbed away the lipstick
his mom left on his cheek
eons ago.

He collapses in front of me,
        hand gripped around the note & the application.
                Moth, honey, I am so sorry. I am so, so sorry.

I swallow hard.

I pull the cigarette from his mouth
& I put my hands firmly on his cheeks.
You have to want to take care of yourself, Sani!
                I can't keep convincing you!
                        Leave me alone!
& I leave.

BUT I COME BACK

I feel pulled too tight;
I find my way back
to Sani's front door
& when he sees me

he holds me like
he will never ever
let me go again.

OUR FOURTH WORLD

We go on a night hike—
           it is cooler, but the bugs hum too loud.

Sani says, *You look different,*
           happy, blurry around the edges.

I say, *You look different,*
           buzzing, thrumming like a guitar string.
Is this the Glittering World?

Sani says, *I hope so. This is where I want to stay.*
           I am going to audition. I am going to try, Moth.

SANI: PEOPLE STAY AWAY

We stay far away
            from the ring of fire,
blazing with people gathered.
We stand near a dry bush,
            silent as snow hiding
from the sun.
Ends & strands of conversations
            drift toward us . . .
            So much for getting help.
Sani turns away.
His lava hair falls in his face
            & I am glad he decided not to cut it.
But then there is music
& Sani's eyes brighten.
            You should practice,
                go play something, I say. *I'll wait here.*
Sani rocks on his heels,
steps toward the fire.
He is offered a guitar
& he plays
& sings in a
language I don't know
while I dance
in the shadows.

I STILL DON'T KNOW WHAT THE (MYSTERY) PILLS ARE FOR . . .

What are the pills for, Sani?

I have a waterfall in my mind.

Should you take the pills, Sani?

& sometimes it pours over my eyes.

Want me to get your pills, Sani?

& makes the world tilt different.

Why are you crying, Sani?

More colorful, more vast.

Let me hold you, Sani?

They are for my mind.

I wonder why he threw them away (again) then.

SANI'S DAD INVITES US
TO DINNER

To yell at us
while clutching the cloth of pills—
      the ones Sani threw away.
Tell her, whoever she is, that you need these. Sani translates.

Tell her that if she cares about you,
she will make you take them, Sani translates.
Why is she so different
      from the others? Sani's dad yells.

Sani takes the pills.
Throws them back
in the trash.
      She's worth it!

You can't audition acting like this!
his dad says.

Sani stands.
I stopped playing when you
left me.
I started singing again
because of Moth!

She makes you sicker, Sani!

   Can't you see how you avoid the world?

His dad storms out the front door,

which swings back & forth

& back & forth

even though

there is no breeze.

WE HAVE A MOMENT
OF SILENCE

Sani's dad is gone for
    one
        six
            ten breaths
before he rushes back in
& stands in front of us
like he has seen a ghost.

SKETCH ME

Sani's dad slams the table.
   I feel the earthquake of it in my spirit.
He scrambles around the kitchen
   until he finds a pencil & a paper.

He says, *Does she know you can draw?*
   Sketch her, Sani.

Sani holds the pencil,
smiles at me through blurry eyes
& begins.

& I don't
& I don't
& I don't
understand why sketching
makes him cry.

SANI'S DAD IS A MEDICINE MAN
WHOSE FATHER KNEW
A HOODOO MAN

Sani's dad opens a drawer,
cradles a photo between
his shaking hands
like a precious offering
before he gently places
the image on the table
next to Sani's sketch.

      My fingers grow toward it.
Sani's fingers beat me to it.
      Why do you have a photo of Moth? he asks.

                   Sani's dad whispers:
                    Her grandfather
                      gave it to me
                    a long time ago.
                  She feels different
            because this was planned.
                This is Hoodoo work.

I stare at the photo; flat
against the oak,
my gray-bearded grandfather's
hand atop my head, smiling—
making his wrinkles deeper.

His father turns the photo over—

        My friend, I know I ask too much,
but if your son can help her home,
she'll teach him how to live.

I don't know how Grandfather knew
I would run away with a boy
with waterfall hair
& campfire eyes.

GRANDFATHER LEFT
A LETTER FOR ME

You will have trouble crossing
from here to there.

Such is often the way with crossings,
but you can't stay here, in your cocoon.

Moth, you must live big,
grow sturdy wings
that can fly you
to a different sky.

I hear Grandfather chanting—
The ancestors are with you, Moth,
            you are never alone.
                    I taught you. You have magic in your bones.
                            Open your eyes, open your eyes,
I would never leave you trapped—defenseless.

Go to the crossroads
            & walk north home.

THE ROOT OF THE ROOT

I look up: *I don't understand—*
    home is east.

                                    Sani's face fractures.
                                      He rips at his hair.
                                            How dare he.
                                                He yells.
                                            How dare he.

I am wispy,
on the verge of fainting.
I don't understand.
Please explain.

                               Sani's dad grabs Sani,
                   who crumbles like a landslide into him.

                       His dad cries, *He knew you had a gift.*
                           He knew what would happen.
                                 If I did not agree,
                            she would have roamed forever
                  & you would have folded inward into nothing.
                         I never thought it would work.

I am fragile,
on the verge of running.
I don't understand.

Sani heaves & looks up at me:
        I can't breathe.
        I can't breathe.

I feel gone,
like a shadow.
I don't understand.

But Sani keeps crying.
I want to reach for him,
but he slips through my fingers.

HUMMINGBIRD MOTH

Sani is the moon & something keeps me
from fluttering to him—
I am trapped in a jar,
watching Sani
storm & wail
in his father's arms.

His father says,
One day the five finger grass
appeared on your skin.
Like an omen.

Sani lifts his head,
eyes darting,
he reaches out
for my hand,
but he can't seem to grasp it.
Moths are both omens
& miracles.

My scar inches open
& open

& open.

& OPEN

There was a crash
 & the car split in two
  & we fell out
   like sticky centers
    of candy bars.

& OPEN & OPEN

Sani's face is fracturing;
        fault lines collect
        as though an earthquake
has erupted somewhere deep in him.

I am being selfish.
You have to leave, Moth.

Is your father mad?

You have to leave.

I don't have a way home.

You have to leave, Moth.

But I love you?

& OPEN & OPEN & OPEN

Sani breaks at the knees
& hits the ground.

                    You're my heart, Moth. (Sani hits his chest.)
                            I love you, but you have to leave.
Why?
(I think I know why.)
              Because you're not real, Moth—your ashes are in a vase.
I am right here.
(I sometimes float away,
I sometimes misplace entire weeks.)
                                    You're a ghost.
I said I won't leave you.
(I'll haunt you if you let me.)
                                 You have to leave.

"Summer Song" lyric: *Darling, let me haunt you.*
                    "Summer Song" lyric: *Honey, I can't.*
                           There is a whole lot of heaven
                                  waiting for you.

TRUTH

Call

me

(Moth)

*

Call

me

(GHOST)

MOTH:

a) nocturnal butterfly
b) night hunter
c) ghost

(Moth) There is a whole lot of heaven
waiting for you.

—Gray-Bearded Grandfather
(Rootworker)

THIS MORNING . . .

I woke up dead.

I WOKE UP DEAD

I Woke Up Dead
     I Woke Up Dead
I Woke Up Dead
     I Woke Up Dead
I Woke Up Dead
     I Woke Up Dead
I Woke Up Dead
     I Woke Up Dead
I Woke Up Dead
     I Woke Up Dead
     I can't understand
why my chest keeps thinking
it has to move up & down—

               if I am already

           gone

               gone

                    gone.

HOODOO FABLE

I woke up dead,
intention gone wolf.

I fell into the wind & let it support
   the soles of my weightless feet.

I forgot every spell, I braided my hair,
I grew it out, green & terrible.

Everything moves to ash in my mouth.

I kept morning rituals (wash, brush, talk),
   but no one *saw* me.

I accidently haunted Aunt Jack.

I picked up things that are not easy
to drop.

A life. A boy.
Things from which I can't loosen my grip:
a boy who my Hoodoo grandfather
knew had a gift for seeing the dead.

No one tells you
you can fall in love
for the first time
                when you are already
                        gone.

SPHINX MOTH

Sani is precise. He sees
past the veil.
He sees me.

I gasp for air I don't need:
                No one ignored me
                        because no one saw me.

No one sees the sphinx next to the trio
of giant pyramids.

I've been entombed
in the dirt.
Covered in dust,
growing wings
only to leave?

TRUTH: ACCIDENT.

When the car split in half like a candy bar
& we (Mom & Dad & brother & I)
fell onto the pavement like sticky filling,
we all made it to the hospital.

Aunt Jack prayed & prayed, but there
was only enough prayer for one of us to walk out.

(Only Aunt Jack walked out.)

My wild heart didn't think it could die.
So I stayed
& punished myself
for living.

& now I can't stop falling
falling
falling.

SANI FINDS (GHOST ME)

I see ghosts.
>Like me.
Nothing like you.
>Like me?
Not alive. But nothing like you.
>That is why you left here?
Yes.

>That is what the pills are for?
>Why your mind is always busy?
>Why you always feel so heavy?
Yes. I feel all the sadness.
>Music helps?
Music abandoned me
until you came along.
>Will you miss me?
Yes.

>Will you audition?
Promise.
>Do I have to go?
Yes.

>No.
Yes. Honey, yes. I am so sorry.

DRIVE TO THE CROSSROADS

It turns out
         when you step out of a cocoon,
you can step out
less alive
but light enough to fly.

It turns out
there is enough
magic & love
in the universe
to mold
your own death mask
but not fully die.

(MOTH) NATURAL HISTORY

It's never the song.
It's the movement of gray notes stacked
   over dark matter.

My voice a whisper to everyone except myself.

Is there a light? A moon to follow, farther down in my center.

Or am I walking away from myself?

Is this the leaving,
   or the staying,
      or the long, long goodbye?

How does one remember how to die?

GRANDFATHER AT THE CROSSROADS

Gray & bearded & hopeful,
Grandfather appears
through the haze, saying,
                    I told you, the dead don't leave.
It is brighter than bright,
            warmer than warm
& I still want to stay
with the boy who is often
as silent as a seahorse.

A boy who sees the dead.
A boy with a violin voice.
A boy who sees me.
Me.
Me.
Me.
(Moth.)

MISSING . . .

      Some mystical red string
stitched up the length of my spine
holds me in two places.

My spirit has been looped
with Sani's.

& I don't know
how to unstitch.

I don't know how
to unravel this magic.

With each step away,
holes pock my soul.
My sphinx moth wings
flutter dusty golden glitter.

I say, *Sani, when you sing*
     I'll dance,
     I'll hear you,
         somehow.

THERE IS A WHOLE LOT
OF HEAVEN

I need to go
to the Fifth World—
         the one that only ghosts know—
with my grandfather,
mother, father, brother
& all the ancestors.

Where death is just one dimension,
one reality,
in a universe of thousands.

So I reach,
weightless
& touch
my grandfather's outstretched hand
         & Sani lets go of mine
         & I flutter my new dusty wings
wide, spotted & brilliant.
& Grandfather tugs me across.

Grandfather says,
Leaving is the hard part.

I collapse into my gray grandfather.
         Will I always have my dusty wings?

Grandfather gathers me closer.

        You grew them yourself, Moth.

They are yours forever. You can always hover.

Behind me in fog & sand

        Sani is on his knees,

forgetting how to breathe, singing,

        If I remember to sing, to live . . .

        Honey, please haunt all my dreams.

SANI: GOODBYE NOTE

I place it in the ground
          in Central Park
so the trees & seeds know
that, to me, you were alive,
'cause spirits do not die—
          they shift.

To me you are alive,
somewhere dancing
          to our "Summer Song."

          & I hope the roots,
the magic, your ancestors
get this message to you
across space
          across time
                    in a place
                              where we find each other (again)
                              in a Sixth World that we create.

Where we live in a cocoon,
          backs laced together along the spine,
                    each of our bodies a wing
                              so when we are born again,
                                        we are one, never to part
                                                  & we can fly & sing
                                                  & dance.

We are one, just you (Moth) & me (Sani)—
Goodbye,
        honey,
                goodbye …

TEN YEARS LATER

Sold Out: Madison Square Garden

Sani: *This song is for Moth.*
   The reason I remember my voice
& try to live, live, live.

"SUMMER SONG"
A gift, an iron to smooth the creases
     that wrinkle up your spirit.
A bundle of beer, a bouquet of clichés
because it's almost summer & it feels right.

In the South we never come empty-handed
& I am nothing if not polite.
I leave courage & cleverness behind
because I am nothing if not polite.

Honey, all the clocks are against us,
   we've got one summer, I'll do your bidding.
Just tell me what you want. I'll do anything you want.

I want to suffocate your sadness,
I want you to run away with me,
please run away with me.

I have found that the whites of your bones
are so lovely, they should be carved into piano keys.

Stars, fireflies in the sky, flicker on & the moon
is a hooked fingernail beckoning us away.

Honey, all the clocks are against us,
            we've got one summer, I'll do your bidding.
Just tell me what you want. I'll do anything you want.

Voltage on our tongues, glows ballerina-witchcraft.
Your hands are fluent in foreplay—
                        all curves & a little bite.
Honey, you can keep me forever, like a phantom limb.

Darling, let me haunt you.
There is a whole lot of heaven waiting for you.
            Honey, please haunt all my dreams.

Honey, all the clocks are against us,
            we've only got one summer,
                    I'll do your bidding
                            just tell me what you want.
                                    I'll do anything you want . . .

Moth: *I grew these dusty wings myself.*
                    I can hover here
                              whenever I want—
                                        Me (Moth).
                                                  Me (Moth).

NOTES

Thank you to my aunt Debbie McBride, a proud member of the Navajo Nation who was kind enough to help me develop the character of Sani. She also helped me to articulate correctly the Navajo myths and creation stories in this novel in verse.

When enslaved Africans arrived in the United States, they were no longer permitted to practice their own spiritual traditions—Christianity was forced on them. Hoodoo is a magic system that grew out of that misfortune, created in the South during slavery. At its core, Hoodoo is a melding of West African spiritual traditions and Christianity. Often referred to as Rootwork, Hoodoo's ultimate goal is to shift the odds in your favor through ancestral worship, offerings, and work with herbs and plants.

Though it is practiced differently from region to region, at the root, Hoodoo highlights the strength and power of the ancestors. Hoodoo is neither good nor bad; it is balance. With the Great Migration, Hoodoo took hold throughout the United States.

MOTH & SANI'S
ROAD TRIP PLAYLIST

1. "My Body Is a Cage," Arcade Fire
2. "Monster 2.0," Jacob Banks
3. "Shrike," Hozier
4. "Sweet Beautiful You," Stateline
5. "Strange Fruit," Nina Simone
6. "Lungs," Jake Howden
7. "Samson," Regina Spektor
8. "Where I Want to Go," Roo Panes
9. "In a Sentimental Mood," Duke Ellington and John Coltrane
10. "All My Life," Texada
11. "Lover, Don't Leave," Citizen Shade
12. "I'll Be Seeing You," Billie Holiday

ACKNOWLEDGMENTS

I started writing this book two months after my own gray-bearded grandfather, William McBride, passed away. My grandfather never missed a birthday, a graduation, or any accomplishment, big or small. Knowing that he was not going to witness my first book in bookstores left a hole in me.

When on February 22, 2019, I climbed into my freezing car to attend Grandfather's funeral, my passenger seat was blazing warm and stayed warm for the entire three-hour car ride. So many people attended his funeral. Every overflow area was used, and people stood outside. On the way to the burial site, the police had to shut down parts of downtown Alexandria—we zoomed pass stoplight after stoplight, and I swore I saw younger versions of Grandfather walking briskly on the sidewalk. Later, coins kept showing up on Grandfather's headstone and I started to remember the stories of Hoodoo I'd heard when I was younger. Writing this book was a healing and a homecoming. So, first and foremost, I must thank my gray-bearded grandfather and the ancestors for always leading me back to center—I've only ever been brave because I want you to be proud of me.

To my parents, Mario and Debra, thank you for your unwavering and unyielding support. Mom, thank you for letting me dream and name trees. Thank you for being my lifelong first advocate, first reader, and voice when mine shakes. Dad, thank you for the thousands of bedtime stories about growing up in Alexandria, Virginia. You taught me storytelling before I could read. Thank you for your steady calm and for killing all the spiders and saving all the mermaids.

Debbie McBride, thank you again for helping me develop the character of Sani. I'll never forget the time I spent when I was younger on the Navajo reservation. It helped craft me into the person I am today. Thank you most of all for being so generous with your history and stunning traditions.

To my wonderful agent, Rena Rossner, you are a lighthouse in my creative world. Because of you, I am not afraid to try new things in writing. I can travel far from shore knowing you will guide me back. Thank you for consistently supporting my own authentic voice. I hope we bring many more books into the universe.

To my editor, Liz Szabla, thank you for seeing Moth so clearly from the start. Thank you for your tireless work and attention to detail; it has been a joy working with you. Many thanks to the entire team at Feiwel & Friends, and a special thanks to Jean Feiwel for allowing me to be a part of this family.

A thousand times thank-you to all of the poets and novelists whose books shaped me as a writer: Jericho Brown, Nikki Giovanni, Toni Morrison, Terrance Hayes, and Tracy K. Smith, just to name a few. I saw my reflection in your books and therefore found my voice.

A particularly special thank-you to Dr. Joanne Gabbin and the Furious Flower Poetry Center for giving me a place to grow and work at a pivotal time in my life. I can never repay the kindness and opportunities you granted me. My gratitude stretches past the boundaries of the known universe.

To my favorite poetry professors, Laurie Kutchins (James Madison University) and John Skoyles (Emerson College). Laurie, thank you for encouraging me to pursue my MFA, and John, thank you for being the reason I thrived in my MFA program.

To the most exquisite human souls, Monica DiMuzio and Cristian Dennis. Monica (middle-school bestie, college roomie, travel buddy, and fellow avid reader), I would not be where I am without you. You make me a better person, thank you. Cristian, thank you for late-night adventures, dance parties, and movie nights. I have always wanted a brother, and the universe sent me you. You are brave and extraordinary and I heart you forever.

The most respectful "hello" to my very large extended family around the world! Thank you for the messages, the phone calls, and the lipstick-stained kisses at church revivals every August. In short, thank you for following my lifeline so closely and for your endless support.

To the younger generation, a much less formal "haiii" to my sister, cousins, and friends: Meghan, Ron, Nimah, Hyison, Summer, Heather, Kiya, Asja, Brandon, Brian, Kennedy, Taja, Norhan, Allison, Abby, Shuruq, Jamar, Ally, and Miya. I know life has led us all to different places, but I'd be remiss if I did not write your names.

Much love to my fur baby and first listener, Shiloh, who has listened to me read her this book a hundred times. Thank you for teaching me stillness for the past eleven years.

To anyone I missed, I see you, I love you.

And lastly to you (readers), thank you for picking up this book. I offer you *a gift, an iron to smooth the creases that wrinkle up your spirit.* Please know that I am always wishing you wellness and joy.